AF819619

Knight Owl

Darcy Flynn

Paper Moon Publishing
Cover Design by Rae Monet, Inc.
Book Design by Jesse Gordon

Acknowledgement Page

I want to thank my dear friend, fellow writer, and now editor, Jeanne Hardt for squeezing me into her busy schedule. Your skilled insights and suggestions made my story even better.

Cindy Brannam, I *so* appreciate your critique, thoughtful suggestions and for catching those pesky typos. You went above and beyond for me this time—thank you, thank you. And Joy Allyson, thanks so much for your thoughtful feedback.

As I developed my plot around a high school principal, I called on Susan Johnson, gifted educator and longtime friend for insight into that world. The results of our brainstorming session are peppered throughout the story. Thanks friend.

To my creative team, Rae Monet for coming out of retirement to make one more gorgeous cover for me, to Karen Duvall for creating the flat and Jesse Gordon, formatter extraordinaire—thank you all.

Finally, thanks to my beautiful readers...for your encouragement and patience during my writing hiatus. You are the absolute best.

It's been a tough two years. I want to thank those of you who've held me up in prayer during this season of great loss. You know who you are. Thank you for your love and support.

For
My beloved son
Roman Seth
You are missed every
moment of every day
In loving memory

CHAPTER 1

Amanda drummed her fingers along the desk at Anna Delany's modeling agency, her stomach in knots. To still her jitters, she took the opportunity to update Like No Other's webpage but gave up after the third attempt. She lowered the lid on her laptop and sat back.

The rumors she'd heard that Jeff Keller, the superintendent of schools, was trying to hire her ex-boyfriend for one of the summer workshops troubled her. As high school principal, she'd have no choice but to work with Ethan. The thought of engaging him in *any* capacity was unacceptable.

Ethan had come back two months ago...*again*. She'd assumed he'd rush in and out, as usual, but this time, he'd stayed. Since he returned to Apalacha Key, she'd made every attempt to avoid him. Oh, she'd spotted him plenty—couldn't help to in a town this small.

But speak to him?

"Not if I can help it," she mumbled.

Due to end-of-school activities, finals, and graduation, she'd escaped the inevitable *run-in*. It wasn't until school ended that eluding him had become more difficult. She knew it wouldn't—*couldn't* last. A weary sigh escaped her lips. It was only a matter of time.

The office phone rang—a welcome diversion to get her mind off Ethan Knight. "Like No Other Modeling Agency," she answered.

"Amanda, Jeff Keller."

Her heart skipped a beat. "Hey, Mr. Keller."

"Good news. I think I've found the guest speaker for our summer journalism course."

Amanda froze, waiting for the inevitable. "W—Wonderful, who did you—?"

"Ethan Knight."

She lifted a hand to her forehead. *So the rumors* were *true*.

"He's in town to sell his family's newspaper and will be spending part of the summer here."

She took a deep breath. Keeping her distance would be impossible if he was hired to teach a workshop. "I thought Mike Simms was in the running for that position?"

"He still is, but this Knight fellow has the most outstanding credentials. Did you know that before his work with the *Orlando Times*, he traveled the world doing exposés for *Geographic World Magazine* and has toured some of the most exotic, amazing, hard-to-reach places on the planet?"

She knew all right and had two photo albums filled with his articles as proof.

"I think the students would love learning from someone who's experienced what he has," Mr. Keller said.

She hoped to steer him in another direction. "I don't see how he can manage the course while working for the *Orlando Times*."

"I understand he only works freelance, now."

"Is that right?"

"Yes, so he should have no problem fitting in the course. He seemed quite pleased about it, too."

I bet he did.

"But sir, I've practically promised Mike Simms the position. You may recall, Mike's taught this workshop the past two summers and expects to lead it this year as well. He's already turned down several other summer opportunities, and I'm not sure he could recover from that at this late date."

"And to pull the rug out from underneath him at this point would be highly unprofessional." At Keller's loud sigh into the receiver, Amanda let out a tightly held breath of her own. She usually assisted the speaker of the journalism course, and no way could she see herself working with Ethan for a single day, much less two full weeks.

"You're right, of course. Simms it is," Mr. Keller said in his jovial manner. "Let him know the job's his, and I'll let Knight know we're going with someone else."

"So, you've already talked specifics with him?"

"Yes, but I'm sure he'll understand."

"Thank you, sir. Mr. Simms is highly qualified and very excited to be working with the students this summer."

"Yes, he is. Now. The only other position we've yet to fill is for the new course on survival skills. I'll have to do some digging. I doubt if anyone local has any knowledge or ability in that area." He paused. "What about you? As I recall, you've had some experience."

"My stint as a Girl Scout leader was limited to pitching a tent in my back yard and making s'mores by the fire." She chuckled. "Neither of which qualifies me for something as serious as survival skills. We could be overreaching with that one, sir."

"Possibly, but we have access to some of the most beautiful terrain in the country—lakes, streams, and all manner of wildlife. I've always wanted to incorporate the surrounding areas into our summer programs. I wonder if this Knight fellow has any contacts in that department?"

Her brain scrambled for an answer as momentary silence filled the space. She'd just dodged a bullet by keeping Simms in the other position only to have another one emerge. Amanda could imagine her boss contemplating the issue—his right hand slowly stroking his chin as he stared off into space —an endearing habit to all who knew the kind, cheerful man.

"It's possible, I guess," she said.

"Well. I'll run that by him when I call."

As she hung up, she thought about how much had changed in their sleepy little fishing village in the past year. Annie and the sheriff were now married, she'd set up LNO's home office there, and then started a modeling agency—all of which brought a bit of notoriety to their community.

Annie's happily-ever-after stood in stark contrast to Amanda's personal life. She used to be comfortable being alone, giving all her focus and time to her career. It wasn't until she'd seen Ethan in the school parking lot seven months prior that her loveless station in life came racing to the forefront of her heart and mind. It had been a long time since she'd allowed herself to think about the day she'd sent him away. As noble as that action was at the time, it had been a terrible mistake. At least, when it came to her happiness.

They say no good deed goes unpunished. Well, she'd been punished all right. The days and weeks she'd waited for Ethan's return had turned into years of disappointment. The pain of that moment had been safely tucked away, deep in the back of the closet of her memories, only to reemerge into the glaring light of regret.

The phone rang again. This time, it was a one of Annie's models asking for clarification on her upcoming photo shoot.

* * *

Ethan's cell phone vibrated on the desk as he finished typing the final sentence on his laptop for his article in *Knight Owl*. He picked up the silver iPhone and pressed the green button. "Knight here."

"Mr. Knight, Jeff Keller. Hope I haven't caught you at a bad time."

"Not at all, and please call me Ethan." He put Keller on speaker and made a hasty correction to the last word on his document.

"I wanted to get back to you about the summer program. It seems the journalism class has already been promised to another individual."

Ethan had no doubt the *said* promise had been given at the hands of Amanda. "Oh, well. No worries."

"I'm really sorry."

"That's okay."

"There is one last position we're hoping to fill, though," Keller said. "It's a two-week survival workshop, which includes an overnight trip in our State Park to apply what the students have learned."

"Really?"

"Yes. I know it's a long shot, but do you have any experience in outdoor survival skills? This would strictly be a beginner course, nothing too outrageous."

"Actually, I do and would be very interested." Ethan

sat back and placed his right elbow on the arm of the desk chair.

"Excellent. And if it goes well, we'll offer another, more-advanced course, in the future."

"Sounds good. I look forward to hearing more about it."

"Great. I'll let Amanda Marsh know. As the high school principal, she'll be your contact person on the course."

"Oh, good. I grew up here," he said. "Amanda and I went to school together."

"Wonderful. I'll have her get in touch with you."

Unable to stop the slow spread of a smile, Ethan pressed *end* and set his phone aside. What he wouldn't give to hear her reaction to Keller's phone call. He knew Amanda and suspected she wouldn't be in any hurry to call him.

It had been seven months since he'd spoken to her. He'd been back and forth many times since then, but had yet to run into her. He'd only seen her at a distance since he'd come back to stay two months earlier. In a town that size, it was obvious she'd deliberately been avoiding him.

Let's see if you can continue to do so when you have to work alongside me at the school.

He'd give her two days, and if he hadn't heard from her by then, he'd simply have Keller set up the meeting. Amanda had and always would obey the rules. If her boss set up the appointment, then she'd have no choice but to meet with him.

He turned his focus back to his computer and read through the article, checking for typos. More importantly, he confirmed the embedded clues so critical to the recipient. Satisfied, he uploaded the new edition of *Knight Owl*, hit publish, then waited for his contact to respond from the other side of the world.

CHAPTER 2

Amanda sat at her office chair, hands clenched in her lap, the only sign of her mounting anxiety. She thought she'd escaped working with Ethan, but her heart took a nosedive upon hearing Mr. Keller had secured Ethan as the survival course instructor. She'd done her best to talk Mr. Keller out of using him, but since she had no other suggestion as to who could take on the course, she'd had no choice but to relent.

She was politeness itself as she nodded in agreement to the scheduled meeting time. Although she ranted and raved internally, she forced a smile and agreed Mr. Knight sounded like the perfect choice for the job.

"I understand Ethan went to school here," Mr. Keller said. "It must be nice to have the opportunity to work with an old classmate."

"Yes, it should be...quite something." She gritted her teeth as Mr. Keller turned and exited her office. As the door clicked shut, she slumped into her chair with a loud huff of frustration.

The months she'd avoided Ethan had been a challenge,

and one she knew would inevitably come to an end. It was one thing to eventually run into him at a restaurant—*that* she'd been prepared for—but to be forced to work with him was unthinkable.

She glanced at the office wall clock. Ethan would be arriving in thirty minutes. She sprang from her chair and made her way to the ladies room. The small mirror over the sink reflected her stormy expression. Face pinched and lips white from grimacing, she rested her hands on each side of the sink and sucked in a deep, calming breath.

Ethan can't see me like this. I must calm my nerves. She inhaled deeply, but the exhale was anything but calm.

Fine. I'll just have to face him as is.

Back in her office, she pulled open the desk drawer and snatched up a rubber band, then twisted her hair into a severe bun at the back of her head. That done, she applied red lipstick, then positioned her tortoise-shell eye glasses onto the bridge of her nose. To finish the façade, she pulled a file folder from the corner of her desk and had it at the ready.

Only a matter of minutes passed when she heard the deep resonance of his voice at the front desk asking for directions to her office. Even after seven months, his voice still sent a ripple of awareness through her. After that run-in, she knew he had come to town on occasion to check on his family's newspaper, but even then, she'd rarely caught a glimpse of him.

Heart in overdrive, she quickly opened the folder, reached for a pencil, and with a tilt of her chin gave her best impression of being deeply absorbed with the contents.

At the light tap on her door, she lifted her head to meet Ethan's focused regard. He entered the office, and the faint, but familiar citrus scent of his aftershave evoked memories from long ago. She caught her breath, as his grayish-blue gaze studied her. She willed herself to maintain her composure, while stilling the rapid beat of her heart.

This was the second time she'd been in close proximity since their confrontation in the school parking lot months before. Fueled by adrenalin, she'd come down on him like a hen protecting one of her chicks. Now, his triumphant expression told her it was *he* who held the upper hand and *she* who felt the sting of reprimand.

She briefly lowered her gaze from the knowing twinkle in his eye as if he, too, had been thinking of that moment. With a number-two lead pencil in hand, she sucked in a steadying breath and looked up at him. "So. The big fish has returned to the little pond." She twirled the yellow pencil between her thumb and index finger. "The shark tank too much for you?"

"Speaking of sharks, I see you've fine-tuned the art of cutting someone down to size since I last saw you." An easy smile played about the corners of his mouth. "Seems this job has gone straight to your head. Makes me wonder what happened to that sweet, little teenager I left behind."

"She. Grew. Up."

"Tell me, are you this prickly with all the men in your life, or is it just me?"

"There are no men in my life." Horrified, she sucked in a breath, appalled at her own words—the raw humor in his eyes brought heat to her cheeks. "Except for one, that is." She lifted her chin.

"And do you provoke him, too?"

"I do not."

"Pity."

"What's that supposed to mean?" *As if it's any of his business.*

"You'll figure it out." He smiled. "Speaking of provoking...

How does it feel to have failed in your attempt to keep me from leading a summer session here at the school?"

With one finger, she pushed her glasses farther up her nose. "Hardly that." She leaned back in her chair. "At least in this program, I won't have to work alongside you, whereas, I would have during the journalism course." She smiled sweetly. "I consider that a win." She pointed the yellow pencil toward the chair opposite her desk.

* * *

Ethan took the seat, slowly and deliberately, allowing himself time to better gage her reaction to his presence. His thoughts went to the day she'd confronted him outside of the school just after he'd questioned Anna Delany about her relationship with the sheriff. Amanda had swooped upon them like a lioness protecting her cub. Chin high, chestnut hair flowing freely about her shoulders—she'd pinned him with her amber stare just like she was doing now.

He deliberately let his gaze linger over her severe and unflattering topknot—pulled tightly from her oval face. The schoolmarm act didn't suit her one bit. Her chest heaved as she inhaled, her nostrils flaring. After a moment, she focused her attention on the open folder and scribbled something on the sticky note.

"What part of, *I don't wish to work with you*, do you not understand?" she bit out.

He openly smiled, ignoring the sting. "Oh, I understand perfectly." He leaned back and made himself comfortable. "But I'm afraid you'll have to take your complaint up with the school superintendent. He offered me the job, and I took it. It's as simple as that."

She snapped the file shut and sat back in her chair. "Why?"

"You don't mince words." He looked directly in her eyes and rested his hands loosely in his lap. "Must be the school principal in you."

She folded her arms, continuing to scowl at him. "And like any good principal, I will not let my question go unanswered."

He moved slightly forward in his chair, clasping his hands in front of him. "I'm thinking about moving back permanently and thought this might be a good way to demonstrate my interest in the community."

Her tawny eyes widened a fraction, then narrowed with a glint of skepticism. "Since when are you interested in anything except yourself?"

Her vitriol caught him off guard, and he leaned back. "Another accusation, or is it the same one you keep hinting at?" He spoke softly, hoping to ease her apparent anger. Her eyes lowered to somewhere around his chest. "That said, you'd be surprised at what I've become interested in since I left home."

His cool, disapproving, reprimand brought a pink stain to Amanda's cheeks. Her slight, uncomfortable shift in the chair told him he'd scored a point.

"As I'm sure you already know," he continued, "I'm home for at least the summer. My family's newspaper isn't doing well and—"

"I'm surprised you haven't sold it already," she shot at him. "Gotten out while you still can. Severing once and for all your connection to this community."

He shook his head. She sure didn't stay down long. "Which I very well may do, but in the meantime, I'm here to discuss the survival course. Since you and I are supposed to work together—"

"Let me make one thing perfectly clear." Her flush grew

deeper, and she adjusted the rim of her glasses. "You and I will *not* be working together." She placed her fingers on a single sheet and slid a form toward him. "Your guidelines for the course. You are the guest instructor, and it is your responsibility to design it. You will then run it by me for approval."

"And if it doesn't meet with your approval?"

"I think you're smart enough to figure that out on your own." She settled against the back of her chair with exaggerated casualness.

"I see." He took the form, rolled it up, then stood. He walked to her side of the desk, forcing her to turn toward him. He stopped, towering over her. Amber eyes fluttered at his nearness. With his right hand on the edge of her desk, he placed his left on the arm of her chair and leaned forward. Her eyes widened, and she shrank back. He glanced from her topknot to the stubborn compression of her lips, then resettled his gaze on her flushed face.

A smile tugged the corners of his mouth. "I have to say, this whole sexy, librarian thing is starting to grow on me." He straightened and moved toward the door. "I look forward to your verdict, *Miss* Marsh." He tapped the rolled paper to his forehead and strode from the office without a backward glance.

CHAPTER 3

Ethan opened his laptop the next morning to find a response to his latest *Knight Owl* submission.

Suspicious activity—current mission postponed—will need to meet in person in the coming weeks.

He rested his elbows on the desk and steepled his fingers against his mouth. Maybe it was time to bring the sheriff into the picture. Weeks earlier, he'd spoken with Levi on the phone, but Ethan wanted to square things face to face, and this would be the excuse he needed to call on him.

After Ethan made his daily appearance at the newspaper, he drove to Sonic for a quick bite to eat. He scarfed down his burger, then made his way across town. Minutes later, he clipped up the steps to the Apalacha Key Sheriff's Department.

Once inside, he only had to wait a few minutes before he spotted the sheriff coming down the hallway. He stood as Levi approached.

"Sheriff Hawke."

Ethan took Levi's hand and shook it.

"I appreciate you coming," Levi said, "but if this is what I think it's about, then it really isn't necessary. Like I told you on the phone, what you printed was the truth and public record."

"Thank you," Ethan said. "I appreciate that, but I wanted to apologize to you personally. And...there's something else I'd like to talk with you about."

Levi's expression turned serious. "Come with me."

Ethan followed him to a small corner office at the end of the hallway.

"Coffee?" Levi offered.

"No thanks." Ethan took a seat on one of two black, vinyl chairs.

Levi took the chair opposite, giving Ethan his full attention. "What's up?"

"I'm involved in something, and I wanted you as sheriff, to be aware of it."

Levi sat back, pressed his fingers together, and regarded him with a speculative gaze. "I'm listening."

* * *

Amanda sat at the front desk at Like No Other with her chin in hand. It had been slow that afternoon, giving her way too much time to think. On impulse, she jumped up and began straightening the fashion magazines on the console table at the entrance.

She'd met the founder, and celebrity model, Anna Delany, seven months earlier when she'd held one of her LNO workshops at Apalacha Key High School. As the school's principal, Amanda's summer hours were shorter, so when asked if she could help out from three to five, she'd jumped at the chance to do something new.

LNO's office mirrored Annie in every way, from the sky-blue, pink, and lavender wool rug to the all-white furniture arranged efficiently to utilize every aspect of the small space.

On the wall behind the white desk hung professional head-shots of some of the models Annie had signed-on since opening the agency four months earlier. A meeting room—which housed a long, rosewood antique table and blue-and-white upholstered chairs—could be accessed to the left of the front desk.

It was such a lovely environment, nothing like her office at the high school with its heavy oak furniture and black desk chair. Even though it rang with function and durability, the true joy of the space was the student's art that she insisted hang throughout the entire suite.

Amanda glanced over the area. Satisfied, she took her seat, placed her elbows on the desk, and sank her chin back in her hand.

"What's up with that face?" Annie entered the office with her arms full of shopping bags.

Amanda straightened. "And what's up with the founder of Like No Other carrying such a load? Why didn't you call me? I'd have met you in the parking lot."

"You need to answer my question first." Annie eyed her closely. "Besides these are light." She deposited half the parcels on the desk and placed the rest on the striped love seat along the sidewall. "They're the LNO backpacks for the next group starting on Saturday."

Annie pulled one out to show her.

"Wow, the girls will love these," Amanda said.

"Especially after we fill them with all the goodies I've gotten donated. But seriously, what's wrong? I know that look." She placed the backpack aside with the others, then sat down in the brightly cushioned wicker chair.

"It's Ethan."

"I see." Annie ran her hand over a wrinkle in her linen skirt, then crossed her legs. "You're not holding a grudge on *our* account are you? Ethan and Levi made peace weeks ago. You do know Ethan's the one responsible for that *New York Post* article about Like No Other."

"Ethan wrote that?" *So, he'd tried to make amends.*

"No, he got one of his New York colleagues, Cameron Phillips, to write it. I think it was his way of saying sorry to us."

"That's wonderful, really. But do you think that fully excuses what he did to Levi?"

Annie lifted her shoulders. "That information was public knowledge, and even though he couldn't retract it, he did apologize for it."

"Well, it'll take much more than some apology article from Ethan to set things right with me. I have my own reasons for holding a grudge, and although what he did to Levi angered me, it's a proverbial drop in the Gulf of Mexico."

"Wow, that sounds like more than a lover's tiff." Annie grinned.

Amanda rolled her eyes. "I can assure you Ethan and I have never been lovers and never will be."

"A childhood sweetheart tiff, then?" Annie's eyes held a twinkle.

Amanda gave her a crushing look.

"Such vitriol," Annie said. "You should see yourself from where I'm sitting. They say hate is akin to love, and I know that from personal experience." She spoke with a confident gleam in her eye. "Care to talk about it?"

"Not really." Amanda lifted one of the backpacks for a closer inspection, deliberately ignoring the *hate-to-love* comment. "Besides, it would take much more time than we have at the moment."

"You two have a long history. Surely there are many happier times for you to focus on."

Amanda's mind whizzed back over the years, then she shook her head as if to rid her brain of the memories. "Of course, there are, but that was then and this is now."

"And Daryl, how does he fit in with all this?" Annie asked.

"There's nothing for Daryl to fit into."

Annie grinned. "You have to put him somewhere in this scenario. I notice you barely ever mention him."

Amanda sighed. "He keeps suggesting we start looking at rings." Something she dreaded and did her best to avoid. Just thinking about it sparked an unpleasant flip in her stomach.

"Wow, that's something I guess." Annie wrinkled her nose. "And what's your response?"

"Truthfully, I always make some excuse why I can't. I do feel a little guilty about that. He knows I'm evading the subject, but he just smiles and says he can wait."

"With your attitude, his *wait* is going to be a long one."

Amanda frowned, and the teasing light disappeared from Annie's eyes. "It sounds like you have a more pressing issue than Daryl."

Amanda nodded and unzipped the side pocket of the backpack. "Mr. Keller expects me to work with Ethan in our newest summer workshop."

"What is it?"

"A two-week survival course."

"That sounds like fun and something I'd like to learn."

"With any other instructor, I would, too." She re-zipped the bag and laid it with the others.

"But not with Ethan," Annie said.

"Exactly."

"Well... I think you should embrace the challenge. If he decides to move back here, you'll be dealing with him at every turn. Why not take this as an opportunity to deal with your Ethan issues, once and for all?" Annie stood, gathered up the backpacks and turned toward her office. "Two weeks is nothing in the scheme of things," she threw over her shoulder as she crossed the room. "And it could be a good test to see if you can put your past with him behind you—get on with your life."

Chin in one hand, Amanda ran a finger along the edge of the desk. "I suppose."

Except, her plan was to veto the course, and the sooner that happened, the sooner he'd sell his newspaper and leave.

CHAPTER 4

The narrow, red-brick two-story building sat on the corner of Market Street and Third Avenue. *Key News* occupied the first floor. Ethan's family still owned the 1940's building, its iconic corner design one of the town's landmarks.

An assortment of large office desks formed two rows throughout the main newsroom. Each cluttered with an individual laptop computer, stacks of paper, personal photos, and an assortment of items particular to the owner. Lime-green office chairs parked at each desk, the only matching furniture in the room. Along the street side, glass windows encased within the oak-paneled doors and walls separated the open floor area from the private offices used by the editors.

Ethan had called this meeting and waited as everyone settled at his or her desk. He checked his wristwatch, then looked out over the somber faces of his employees. Perching his hip on the edge of the desk nearest him, he clasped his hands together. "I'm sure you have questions regarding the future of the paper."

"Are our jobs in jeopardy?" Megan blurted out.

"Megan." The sharp reprimand from Ned cut through the room.

"It's all right, Ned," Ethan said. "Megan's just voiced what I'm sure you're all thinking."

Several glanced back and forth between themselves, their gazes resting again on Ned, the assistant editor, who had been running the paper since the death of Ethan's father.

"Well then," Ned said, "is there anything you can tell us about the paper's future? This is our livelihood, and frankly, we're on pins and needles as to what your plans are."

"I understand," Ethan said. "I'm fully aware this is a stressful time for all of you. I'll soon have several options to consider, all of which will include either merging or selling the paper. Hopefully, you'll be able to keep your positions here, but if not, I can assure you I'll make certain each one of you receives a good severance package." Low murmurs peppered throughout the room. "This process will likely take most of the summer to complete, so don't start cleaning out your desks yet." He smiled, hoping his comments added some levity to the situation. "As I get new information, I'll certainly let you know."

He stood and stuffed his hands into his pockets. "You're all doing a great job, and I know my father would've been very proud of you. As you can imagine, this is also tough on my grandmother, but my life, at this time, doesn't lend itself to running a small-town newspaper."

He gazed at the serious faces staring at him. "Carry on." He dismissed everyone and walked through the aisle between the desks toward the exit.

He hadn't yet decided on the paper's future, but hoped he'd given them enough information to keep them focused on the job at hand. Having promised his grandmother that he'd give a real effort to the paper's future, he'd hired a newspaper broker. John Duncan knew of several media conglomerates that might be interested but hadn't yet called with anything concrete.

Truthfully, he'd come home with the intention to sell and get out. The day Amanda confronted him in the high school parking lot with that haughty tilt of her chin, her enchanting, school-principal glare had changed everything. In that moment, his feelings for her rushed back full force.

At that time, his work schedule hadn't allowed him to stay, but he'd been determined to return as soon as circumstances permitted. He was back now and ready to give their relationship one more chance.

He exited the building and squinted against the noonday sunshine. He slipped on his aviators and climbed into his BMW. The night before, he'd planned out the two-week survival course, culminating with an overnight camping trip in Apalacha Key State Park.

He'd learned a great deal of survival skills while traveling to faraway destinations for *Geographic World Magazine.* Far more than what would be needed or expected in his beginner course.

He'd put the finishing touches on the document that morning. He knew Amanda planned to veto the course. Her attitude and actions made it clear she had no intention of working with him. Even so, he hoped it would meet with the superintendent's approval, and believed if it did, she'd have to comply with his wishes.

Minutes later, he pulled into the parking lot of the high school, ready for battle.

* * *

Ethan tipped his head toward the framed documents on the wall behind Amanda's desk. "One can't help but notice *all* those diplomas," he said. "You were always such an excellent student."

She had been ready for him when he walked into her office, but his remark caught her off guard. "Education is my first love." She smugly smiled.

"Principal at twenty-eight." His gaze remained focused on the wall behind her. "You've certainly fast-tracked the process. That must have been difficult."

"It's a simple case of knowing what one wants to do at an early age, and then going for it." She folded her hands together, resting them on top of the desk. "After earning my masters in educational administration, I received my Principal Certification online."

"I thought you had to have *years* of experience teaching to become principal of a high school. Most school principals are middle-aged and graying at the temples."

"Apparently, five years teaching English was sufficient for this district. That said, don't be too impressed. I wasn't the school district's first choice but the one who finally said, *yes.* It seems *small-town* life just isn't for everybody."

"Apparently."

She gathered the loose papers in front of her and placed them neatly to the side. "Now, if we can dispense with the third degree, I'd like to get down to business."

He took the chair opposite the desk and handed her the document.

Amanda slipped on her eyewear and reluctantly scanned the proposal. "*The six basic survival skills. Planning ahead, fire, shelter, signaling, first aid, and food and water.*" She lowered the document and stared at Ethan. "That's seven."

"Food and water are under the same heading. We can rename it, sustenance, if you'd like."

She lifted the document. "So, this is it?"

"No, that's the cover page. There's more detail on the following pages."

She flipped over one page, then another. "What's signaling?" she glanced back at him.

"It allows you to make contact with people when you need help," he said. "There're a variety of ways...fire and smoke—"

"You mean like smoke signals?"

"Yes. One can also use whistles, flashlights, and several other ways if you'd care to *read* the document."

She nodded and deliberately took her time to peruse the rest of the pages.

After a few moments, she heard Ethan expel a long breath. "I hope the course meets with your satisfaction." His heavy sarcasm came through loud and clear.

She smothered a smile and glanced up. Her gaze met that devastatingly attractive, quirked brow, and the gleam of mockery that always followed when he'd challenged her in the past. His eyes reflected the words that fell from his lips.

She glanced down and briskly stacked the papers neatly in front of her. "It seems to be quite thorough and in order." She took a swift, steadying breath. "Too bad that loathsome *Knight Owl* rag you publish doesn't have the same integrity of substance."

His eyes narrowed to a critical squint. "To you, maybe," he drawled with distinct mockery. "But to others, a lifeline."

She scoffed a laugh. "That's ridiculous." She held up the syllabus. "Thank you for getting this to me in such a timely manner. I'll look it over in greater detail later today when I have more time."

She placed the document aside and folded her hands primly in front of her, intent on ending the session...but he just sat there, which was so like him. He had to know his nearness grated—she'd made it plain enough. She deeply inhaled and focused on the papers in front of her. The sooner he left her office, the better.

"Before I go," he said, "I'd like to set a firm time for our next meeting. According to the summer course schedule, the workshops start two weeks from now. I'm anxious to order supplies for the course."

"A meeting won't be necessary." She shot him a quick, sidelong glance. "I'll respond to you via email. And I'll copy Mr. Keller as well."

When he still didn't budge, she lifted her gaze to his. "I'm sorry, is there something else you wish to discuss?" she snapped.

He slowly stood and regarded her for a moment. "Not a thing. You've made your position perfectly clear."

"I'm glad to hear it. And one more thing..." She pulled off her glasses and fixed him with a stare. "Just so you know, we have to have a minimum of ten students to hold a summer session. The financial investment wouldn't be worth it otherwise."

"And I'm sure you'll do all in your power to make certain the enrollment falls just below what is required," he said over his shoulder as he left.

Actually, she hadn't thought about interfering, but since he'd just accused her of it, she might as well consider it.

CHAPTER 5

Amanda watched Ethan's back as he left her office, doing her best to ignore his wonderful broad shoulders as he pushed through the heavy oak-and-glass door. She'd infuriated him. *Good*. No more than he deserved for the uncontrollable heart palpitations he'd inflicted with his nearness.

He'd been gone for years, and yet he was just as she'd remembered. The young, good-looking college student was gone, but the thirty-year-old replacement was more in every way—more handsome, more dangerous, and more disruptive, especially to her ordered, mapped-out, world.

On the day she'd allowed herself to accept that he was never coming back, she'd pushed forward with her ordinary life, settling in and establishing herself in her hometown. She'd begun dating again, on and off, but no one came close to her darling, Ethan.

Not even Daryl. Sweet, thoughtful Daryl, who'd told her she was everything he had ever dreamed of. Sadly, her heart didn't reciprocate.

Why did Ethan have to reappear, with that heart-tugging

air of arrogant charm? He completely disarmed and upset her with the reminder of all she'd given up for him to succeed.

Oh, why did he have to come back now? She'd finally tucked him and the future they'd planned safely away. Once, he'd meant everything to her. The handsome, all-American athlete had led her from a systematic, structured life to one with the promise of a future filled with love and adventure.

She dropped her face into her hands, the pain of his nearness overwhelming. She'd have to learn to deal with it, especially if he stayed. If she had to work in close proximity with him, it would only be a matter of time before she caved. He could never know her true feelings. She could not endure another heartache at his hands. She shook her head, seeing no other way out of it. She'd have to veto the course, no matter how well-planned and good it was.

She groaned. What she needed was an extra-large scoop of cherry cream cheese ice cream.

* * *

Ethan's long strides had him down the hallway and out the school's massive front doors in less than a minute. Halfway through the meeting, he knew what her verdict would be, even before she'd spoken the words. Well, he'd dealt with a lot worse than the likes of her over the years.

Twenty minutes later, Ethan stood at the entrance of *Key News* where journalists, editors, and reporters swarmed with the activity of a functioning beehive. The low buzz of their voices sounded much like humming bees, and he smiled.

Since he'd arrived, he hadn't once taken the time to watch the process of a newsroom. Although small, each department was still represented—editorial, sales, production, circulation, and marketing. The latter was probably the least efficient, and if changes could be made in that sector there was a good chance the paper would survive, whatever its future.

He made his way to the editor's office, and several staff raised their heads, giving him a friendly nod as he passed their desks. He stepped through the opening and closed the door behind him. He had a scheduled call with John Duncan, the newspaper broker out of Chicago.

Ethan answered the call on the second ring.

"This is a huge step," John said. He'd gotten to the point after a few pleasantries. "*Key News* is a fourth-generation local paper. Are you sure you want to give that up?"

"I'm a photojournalist, not a newspaper man." Ethan switched the phone from his left ear to his right.

"There was a time when they were pretty much the same."

"That was a long time ago, but times have changed." Ethan leaned back in the green office chair. "At least they have for me."

"All right. If you're sure."

"I'm sure."

"Right now, I have several that are looking to merge or buy —I'll get back to you with a couple of options in a day or so."

* * *

Amanda pushed through the glass door of Dairy Delight, the local diner and ice cream parlor. She crossed the black and white checkered floor—straight for the counter. It had been more than fifteen years since the owner had created cherry cream cheese ice cream, and from that time, it had been her go-to comfort food. It had seen her through many school breakups, failed math tests, and adolescent heartbreaks. After her meeting with Ethan, she was in dire need of a scoop. She had thirty minutes before her next meeting at the school—just enough time to soothe her unsettled nerves.

Amanda sat down at the red laminate countertop as Dee Bell greeted her with a broad smile.

"Hey, Dee."

"Hey, Mandy."

Amanda waved away the menu Dee held in her hand. "I know what I want."

"Okay." Dee held the order pad and pen at the ready.

"One large scoop of cherry cream cheese, please."

"Uh, oh." Dee grinned. "Bad morning?"

"The worst."

"Cup or cone?"

"Cup."

"Coming right up." Dee grabbed the ice cream scoop and lowered her hand into the deep container.

"Make that two scoops." Amanda rested her forearms along the edge of the countertop.

"You got it."

A minute later, Dee placed the creamy confection in front of Amanda, then gave her attention to another customer at the far end of the counter.

* * *

Ethan left *Key News,* and as he was about to pass Dairy Delight, he spotted Amanda at the counter. After a moment's hesitation, he pushed through the glass door.

He sauntered up to Amanda, and she flipped the spoon upside down and slowly pulled it from between her lips. "Still bingeing on Dee's famous cherry cream cheese, I see," he said.

Amanda froze, the empty spoon near her lips. Holding the

utensil in midair, she looked left, and then right. He followed her gaze along the row of the empty counter seats.

"Be with you in a sec," Dee said, giving a last swipe on the table behind him.

"I am not bingeing. I'm de-stressing, as you well know." She eyed him with a critical frown. "And do you have to sit right there?" she asked, as he took the seat next to her.

"I do, actually. Our conversation is not over." He waved to Dee. "I'll just have coffee, please."

He glanced at Amanda—whose expression had turned to one of dismay—and waited while Dee poured him a cup.

After tipping a small amount of cream into the hot, black liquid, he lifted the rim to his mouth. Diner coffee—not the best—but any excuse to torment Amanda was worth it.

The object of his torment turned away and lowered her spoon to the counter.

"Not enjoying your ice cream?" he asked.

"What do you think?" She pulled a few bills from her wallet, tossed them on the counter, grabbed her purse, then stood.

"Are you going to continue running away every time I'm near?"

She halted for a second and leveled him with her *schoolmarm stare*.

"What? You don't think I've noticed you hightailing it in the opposite direction every time you see me?"

For an answer, she continued to stare with her pouty lips pursed tightly together.

"Why don't you sit back down and finish your ice cream like a good girl? It would be a shame to let all that sweet, cherry goodness go to waste." He grinned.

"Sorry, but I've lost my appetite. Besides, I have a meeting in twenty minutes. It's time to get back."

A group of students from the high school noisily clambered into the diner.

He glanced over his shoulder as they settled into a booth. "Unless you'd like a scene in front of your wee lambs, I suggest you sit."

Her eyes widened to enormous proportions as she glanced from him to the students, then back to him. "Excuse me?"

"And stop with the high-school-principal act. I'm not one of your students."

"Fine." Jaw clinched, she hitched her bag over her shoulder and sat. "Say what you want then."

"I can see that you loathe me for *whatever* it is I've done. That said, I'm the only person available with the know-how to teach these kids life-saving, survival skills."

"And just where did you come by these *skills*?"

"Mostly from my travels abroad." He sipped his coffee, then set the cup back onto the saucer. "Won't you set aside your feelings for me and think of them?" He tipped his head toward the students across the diner. As she focused on them, her sudden, semi-relaxed posture signaled she was beginning to relent.

"I have to fully read your proposal before I can decide." She picked up her spoon and shoved a velvety mass of ice cream into her mouth.

Well, at least that wasn't a *no*. Not that it would make much difference, as Keller was the final authority in the matter. It would be a plus if Amanda also agreed. Okay, so he'd apparently hurt her, and far worse than he'd thought. His calls had become less frequent, but so had hers, until one day, neither had made the effort to keep in touch. If her pain had been caused from the mere fact that he'd gotten on with his life after college, then she'd have to just get over it. She'd have no reason to know, but he *had* kept up with her through his grandmother.

She'd obviously built a wall, not only against him, but also toward further disappointment. He understood that, but having a non-hostile rapport with her was an important first step to rekindling their relationship. If he were to have any headway, diffusing her anger would be necessary in order for him to regain her trust.

"I see you've let your hair down." Eyeing her, he dabbed his mouth with the paper napkin. "Nice color. I like it."

"What is that supposed to mean?"

He shrugged. "I just remember it darker, that's all."

She shot him a sidelong glance and shoved another heaping spoonful of the half-melted ice cream into her mouth. That may have stopped the torrent of words he knew she longed to let fly, but the accusations spewing from her sparkling, copper eyes, said it all.

She returned her focus to the dwindling sweet cream and tucked a long, golden-brown strand of hair behind her left ear, exposing the tiny heart-shaped birthmark he used to love to kiss. He propped an elbow on the counter and rested his chin on his fist, curbing the strongest desire to press his lips to that very spot.

He studied her profile, taking in the slight pout of her sweet lips—their sulk growing more pronounced with each spoonful of sweet cream. How many times had he found her there, in that very spot, sad and dispirited after one of their arguments, or from some other schoolgirl disappointment, consoling her pain with the same cherry cream confection?

They'd always worked out their differences—always ended up with a make-up kiss—his favorite part. The rush of memory and of her sugary lips squeezed his heart.

He groaned inwardly, then abruptly stood. "One of these days, I'm going to find out what this antagonistic behavior of yours is all about."

He placed a few bills on the counter. "I can see I've tormented you long enough. I guess I'll just have to pace myself."

She blinked and cast him a confused look. "Pace yourself for what?"

"In giving you time to build up your immunity to my presence."

Chapter 6

The following afternoon, Amanda smiled her approval over Mr. Simms' syllabus on the journalism course. "Excellent, Mike. I think this is even better than last summer's."

"I think so, too." Mike smiled with gratification.

They both stood and shook hands. "So. What assistance will you need from me?" The past three summers, she'd happily assisted Mike with his course. It had been a way to exchange her *principal hat* for that of *teacher's assistant*.

A slight flush crossed Mike's face. "A—about that," he stuttered. "I hope you don't mind, but Lindsay Thomas has asked if she could assist me this year."

"Oh. Well, of course. Lindsay would be perfect. She's had a great first year here, and all the students love her."

Something Amanda interpreted as relief crossed Mike's face. "I agree, the kids really like her. Thank you for understanding, I—"

"Please," Amanda waved a hand, "don't give it another thought."

After Mike left, she made her way to the teacher's lounge,

smiling. Seems it wasn't only the students that *liked* Miss Thomas.

Amanda pushed through the lounge door and surveyed the narrow but ample space. The left side housed one rectangular lunchroom table with six chairs lining both sides. The kitchen wall, consisting of a long counter with upper and lower cabinets, filled the right side. As far as snacks and drinks went, the small but efficient room had everything the teachers could want.

Standing on tiptoe, she opened the upper wall cabinet, grabbed a clean mug, then poured a liberal amount of coffee into the cup.

When she returned to her office, she scribbled out a few notes about her meeting with Mike. She took another sip of black liquid and glanced at the folder holding Ethan's survival course proposal. She'd put off reading it long enough, as if ignoring the proposal could somehow negate their confrontation at Dairy Delight. She heaved a sigh and snatched up the document. The sooner she finished it, the sooner she could veto it.

Twenty minutes later, she sat, tapping her pen against the oak desk. Ethan's class proposal was not only good, but one of the best summer workshop proposals she'd ever read. No way could she veto it. To do so would be more than dishonest—it would go against her personal ethics.

She tossed the pen down and sat back. There had to be another way to stop it from taking place. Once the course description was on their school website, they'd be turning students away. Or heaven help her, adding a second summer session. Too much to hope that the website would be down during the signup week.

She placed her palms to her forehead and blew out a

breath. She was being utterly ridiculous. So what if the class was a raging success? Except for the initial start, she didn't have to work closely with him. And once the course was over, he'd be on his merry way—out of town and out of her life.

* * *

Ethan's cell phone rang while he drove to his grandmother's house for dinner. He clicked on the green dot. "Knight here."

"Ethan, it's John Duncan. I've got that information. Is this a good time to talk?"

"Yes, it is." Ethan put John on speaker.

"Both Granger and Leeds Capital are interested in buying. Granger has two hundred and fifty daily outlets and Leeds Capital has sixty or so."

Ethan slowed his car and turned right. "Anything I should know?"

"I can tell you Leeds is hungry and anxious to acquire more papers. I'll send over the specifics for both. Those should help with your decision."

Ethan slowed at the next corner, put on his blinker, then turned left. "Thanks, but in the meantime, go ahead and set up a Zoom call with Leeds Capital. I'm thinking small might be better for my people."

"Will do."

Ethan ended his call as he pulled into Mel's Market for *something white*...his grandmother had said. He chose a bottle of Sauvignon Blanc, paid the cashier and left. Five minutes later, he turned the car right onto the gravel drive in front of his quaint, family home on 11th Street.

The classic revival cottage had been in his family for two generations. The light-yellow, wood siding welcomed him with its floor-to-ceiling windows, wide covered front porch, and sloping roof.

He drove to the right side of the house, parked the BMW and got out. He pushed through the antique iron gate and made his way to the back entrance.

Spicy aromas filled his nostrils as he stepped onto the tile floor leading into the small blue-and-white kitchen. His grandmother had moved in with him and his dad after his mom died fifteen years earlier. At the time, it was only going to be temporary, but after much cajoling from his father, she'd stayed on.

"Right on time." His grandmother tapped the wooden spoon on the side of the large cast-iron pan, then turned toward him, greeting him with her ready smile. "Have I told you how wonderful it is having you home?"

"Every time I walk through the door." He tossed his car keys on the counter near the wall phone, and then gave her a peck on her upraised cheek.

"And you're going to continue hearing me say it, too. I know your life... How you're never in one place long enough to have a home of your own. It's time you settled down. Have you run into Amanda yet? Believe it or not, she's still single." Spoon, still firmly gripped, she turned back to the simmering dish.

Ethan rummaged through the top kitchen drawer, lifted the corkscrew, and proceeded to open the wine. "As a matter of fact, I saw her today at the high school. I had to meet with her regarding the survival workshop I'm hoping to teach there."

"That's lovely, dear."

After he filled each glass, he pulled one of the pine chairs from the kitchen table. He twisted it around, straddled it, and placed his arms comfortably across the back. "Need any other help?" He didn't know why he asked because she always said, no.

"No. You just sit there and relax. I've got this."

In minutes, she had the spicy shrimp dished up and set before them. He turned his chair around as she took her seat, waited for her to ask the blessing, and then dove in.

"How are things at the paper?" she asked. "You settling in okay?"

She'd timed the question when his mouth was full. He met her guileless expression with a frank one and swallowed. "Grandma, naïve doesn't suit you." He shook his head and smiled. "You're one of the most direct women I know."

He'd planned to give her an update, but not at dinner. Apparently, she couldn't wait. He took a sip of wine, and then forked up more rice and shrimp. "You sure you want to discuss this now?" he asked, holding his fork midair. "I'd hate to give you indigestion." He shoved that spicy morsel into his mouth, scooped up another ample amount, and sunk his teeth into the savory dish. He wanted to enjoy her good cooking, not an acid stomach.

She broke off a piece of French bread and began to butter it. "Yes." She raised her gaze to his. "You know how I feel about the paper. I want to know what's happening. Waiting, day after day, is giving me heartburn."

"It's not like I haven't already made it clear to you. My goal is to sell." He pinched off a piece of warm, crusty bread. "If that doesn't work out to my satisfaction, I'll go to plan B."

"Which is?"

"I'm not sure. Okay?"

She pursed her lips firmly together, lowered her fork, picked up her napkin, and dabbed her mouth.

He reached across the table and placed his hand on hers. "This is going to take time. The merger I'm seeking takes weeks of negotiations. Finding the right fit for our employees, for the community, won't happen overnight. I'll likely be here most of the summer."

"Is there no way to save it?"

He rested his forearms on the edge of the table. "There's not much profit anymore—the paper is barely breaking even."

She grabbed her fork and pushed a lone shrimp across the plate.

"Bringing it up to more modern standards could make it more profitable, I guess, but that would take time and the right company backing it." He lifted a shoulder and bit into the bread.

"But for someone else," she said. "Not you."

He sighed. "At this point in my life... I'm afraid not."

"But why do you have to sell? Why now?"

"Honey, Dad *was* the paper. It was his life. He made it all work—day in—day out. I'm afraid that's not for me."

She sat twisting her hands in agitation. Her gaze held heartfelt appeal. It pained him to see her like that. He knew what the paper meant to her. His great-grandfather started *Key News* in 1934 with only three employees when Apalacha Key was just a small fishing village. Ethan was the fourth generation and wanted nothing to do with it. It had to end sometime. The world was changing, and it was difficult for her.

"Look, I promise to do all I can to take care of our employees. Whether it's in keeping them on or giving each a good severance package. Those are details that will be worked out in due time. We don't even have a buyer yet."

He didn't want to have the same discussion with her every time he walked in the door. He loved his grandmother dearly, but if she kept hounding him at every turn, he'd have to find lodgings elsewhere.

CHAPTER 7

Amanda arrived at LNO's office the following afternoon, and she found Annie setting out the gifts for the goody bags. Mounds of beauty products filled the eight-foot-long workroom table—from lipstick and nail polish, to sparkly compact mirrors and a variety of skincare products.

"This is amazing." Amanda snapped up a slender lipstick tube, and with one twist, unfurled a deep rosy-pink shade. "You got all of this donated?"

"Yes, and this is only half of it. Look inside that cardboard box on the floor. It's full of hair products."

Amanda pulled apart the top flaps of the box and proceeded to organize sample-size bottles of hair spray, shampoo, cream rinse, hairbrushes, and portable hair dryers on the opposite end of the table.

"While you unload all of that, I want to float an idea for a new session," Annie said.

"Okay."

"The title will be, *It's Not All About You*." Annie glanced at Amanda. "What do you think?"

"I like it. So, what'll it entail?"

"That's why I'd like your thoughts. You're with teens months at a time, dealing with all kinds of issues." Annie paused, locking her gaze with Amanda's. "They need to know and understand that not everyone has had the same upbringing, or experiences, and those differences have helped to form who they are today." She shrugged. "I don't know quite how to word it, but teen girls can be really mean and judgmental of their peers."

Amanda nodded as she gathered a bunch of multicolored eyebrow-shaping razors. "Exactly. It's important they not only have respect for others, but they also demonstrate it."

"Yeah, and they need to understand not everyone has had it as easy as they have." She stacked small boxes of eyeshadow compacts to her right. "Most of them are so self-centered, they've seldom thought about what the person sitting right next to them has been through." She shook her head and grinned. "Am I being too serious?"

"I don't think so," Amanda said. "I've seen it over the years working with them. And it's not just the girls, but the boys, too. They can be so quick to label others." She unscrewed the cap on a bottle of cologne. "I like where you're going with this, and I'll be happy to put some more thought into it." She lifted the bottle to her nose and inhaled. "Ooooh, this is nice."

"Yes, that's *Cloud* by Ariana Grande. Once in New York, I asked the girls in my workshop what they wanted in a perfume. They all basically said, they liked girly and fresh and didn't want to smell like they were going to a business meeting."

Amanda laughed, selected an oblong box, and read the inscription on the side. "Wireless Bluetooth portable speaker." She pulled a square, seafoam-green object from inside. "Wow, the girls will love these."

"I know. Sony donated them. Aren't they cute?"

"I'll say."

They finished unloading and organizing the gifts, and Annie tossed her one of the speakers. "There you go."

Amanda grinned. "Thanks."

"Are you kidding? I should be thanking you. Every afternoon, you spend hours helping me and refuse to accept payment."

Amanda shrugged a smiled. "I've had the best time here, really. It's a nice change for me."

"I'm glad, and thanks for any and all insights you come up with for the new session. I just want LNO to really mean something for these girls. I want it to be fun, yes, but with substance...you know?"

Amanda nodded. "Something character-building and for the long haul."

"Exactly," Annie said, sorting the gifts into one of the small, lavender backpacks. "I want them to finish the course with something more than cute little speakers and the latest shade of lipstick."

* * *

Ethan joined Amanda in her office the following morning, to go over the supply list for his survival course.

He flashed her his brightest smile as he entered and took the chair opposite her desk before she could ask him to be seated.

"My, aren't we eager this morning." She cast him a critical eye as he handed her a folder.

"What's this?"

"The list of supplies I'll need for the course."

She ran her gaze over the items and shook her head. "Aren't you just a bit premature?"

"Hardly. The course starts in two weeks."

"Premature," she continued as if he hadn't spoken, "as in, I haven't decided if it will even take place." With a slight tilt of her head, she sat back with exaggerated casualness—as if challenging him with a display of superior confidence.

His gaze locked with her overly confident one, and he smiled, *slowly*. "Are you saying that you're the final authority in this decision?"

"Well, not the final, of course, but Mr. Keller will certainly consider my opinion on the matter." The words had barely left her lips when the object of their discussion walked in.

"Sorry I'm late." Keller glanced at them and pulled up a side chair next to Ethan's. He nodded to Ethan, and then at the stunned faced of Amanda sitting behind her desk.

"Mr. Keller," she said. "I didn't know you'd be joining us this morning."

"Oh, I'm sorry. I assumed Ethan would tell you."

Ethan sent her a bland expression. "I did try to call you, but it kept going to your voice mail."

"A text would have been sufficient... That said..." She focused on Keller. "You needn't stay, sir, as I haven't had a chance to okay the program yet. I still have several unanswered questions. For instance..." She lifted the document and looked pointedly at Keller. "This list of his... There's no way we can get these supplies here on time. We could possibly try again for another course later in the summer—"

"Nonsense," Keller said.

"Sir?"

He waved his hand through the air. "It's all been ordered. Isn't that right, Ethan?"

"Yes, sir." He smiled with satisfaction. "Amanda you may recall, *planning ahead*, is the first survival skill. I realized time was short, and since Mr. Keller assured me it would be a go on your part, as well as his..." He gave a careless shrug. "I decided to place the supplies order, myself."

She pressed her lips tightly together. "I do appreciate your tenacity, but some of this equipment is quite costly, and I'm afraid way beyond our budget."

"No worries on that score, Miss Marsh," Keller added. "Ethan has graciously offered to pay for it all."

"Really?" Amanda bristled but forced a smile for Keller's benefit. "That's so, so...magnanimous of him."

"So, we're all set then?" Ethan asked with feigned innocence. She tossed him a scathing glance, then turned her attention to Keller. Ethan sat back and listened to her last feeble attempt to sway her boss to put off the course indefinitely, listing several reasons.

"Why, it most likely won't even draw the minimum of ten students required," she argued.

"I wouldn't worry about that, since it doesn't matter how many sign up. The amount of students needed won't apply in this instance."

"Won't apply, but sir—"

"Since Knight is paying for the supplies, it won't matter whether it's five or ten students."

As Keller continued to explain, the reaction on Amanda's face was worth every penny he'd spent.

CHAPTER 8

Amanda held herself in check as she watched Ethan and Mr. Keller stand and shake hands.

Mr. Keller made for the door. "Keep me posted, Miss Marsh, on anything else you need for the course."

"Will do, sir."

She waited until Mr. Keller left, then turned her full attention to Ethan. Amusement flickered in the eyes that met hers. Okay, so he'd won that round. *Fine.* He could hold his two-week session with the help of someone other than her. For the student's sake, she would make sure it ran smoothly and without a hitch. But that was all she would do.

She'd already given Jenny Peterson, the girls' P.E. teacher, a heads-up that she would assist Ethan if the course went forward, and as an avid camper, she would be perfect for the overnight finale to put into practice what the kids had learned.

"So. You're paying for all of those camping supplies. How generous of you."

"So you said."

"I said magnanimous."

"Yes, you did."

She snatched up a large textbook from her desk and stepped over to the floor-to-ceiling bookcase on her right.

"Is that what has you so riled up—that I sidestepped your little plan to derail my workshop—that I outsmarted you?"

She snapped her head around, but she held back the angry retort that sprung to her lips, certain he would just love her to lose it with him. In the past, he'd always managed to get a rise out of her as if he alone could control the conversation between them. Not today.

"Sure, you outsmarted me." She carefully slid the book onto the shelf, turned, and raked her gaze over his tall form—an action that brought the amused gleam back into his eyes. "I'd forgotten how *devious* you could be when you want your own way."

"Devious? *Me*?" He cocked one eyebrow and shook his head. "I'm sure that lovely brain of yours spent countless hours planning and plotting and doing all manner of mental gymnastics to thwart my efforts to participate in the summer programs."

Heat rose in Amanda's cheeks, and she dropped her gaze from the blazing confidence in his *I know all about you* stare. Of course, he was right. That was exactly what she'd done. "You think you still know me? Well, you can be certain that I still know you, too."

"I have no doubt that's true." His hands rested on his hips. "But as they say, forewarned is forearmed."

He was doing it again, pushing for a rise out of her. She took a steadying breath and simply posed a question. "Why is it so important for you to teach this course? Why are you really here?"

"I'm here to take care of family business, and to sell the newspaper."

"I know that. I meant *here*, at this school, participating as if you really care."

"I'm sorry." He casually stuffed his hands into his pockets. "Am I not allowed to take an interest in my alma mater?"

She folded her arms and gave him her no-nonsense glare. "Then why didn't you attend our ten-year reunion?"

"I was...indisposed."

"I see. Gallivanting around the world, as usual. Well, everyone missed you. In fact, they kept asking me what you were doing and where you where...as if I would know."

She moved to the front of her desk and sat back on the edge, gripping the sides with her hands. "Sadly, I had to tell them I had no idea *where* you were or *how* you were because I hadn't heard from you in a while, which was, of course, a lie. What I didn't tell them was that I'd *never* heard from you, not once since you went away."

"That's not—"

"That would have been way too humiliating, so I kept that little piece of information to myself. Even so, I still had to endure their soulful, pitying stares. After all, we'd dated all through high school, planned our entire future together, and parted with the promise of only a...*short* separation. That was seven years, nine months, and six days ago, but who's counting?" Her tirade ended on a high-pitched hysteric.

Tears filled her line of vision. Horrified, she blinked them away.

"Mandy, I'm sorry." He stepped toward her. "I—"

"Save it." She pushed off the desk and stepped away.

"No." He placed a restraining hand on her arm. "I'm not

saving it. You've been furious with me since that day in the parking lot. I'm listening now, if you'd like to tell me anything."

He looked her in the eye and waited, but she refused to respond.

"If you have nothing to say, then fine, but don't forget, *you* were the one who sent me away." He held her gaze a moment longer, then dropped his hand from her arm.

She still refused to speak. He gave a quick nod, turned, and in three long strides, walked through the door.

"Mr. Knight."

He stopped, turned his head slightly left, and frowned at her.

"I'll need your complete course outline by Monday, including any other essentials you'll need for the workshop. Any further communication between us will be kept short and to the point. I don't wish to spend any more time with you than is absolutely necessary."

"I understand, Miss Marsh." He gave a salute and left.

* * *

Ethan exited the high school steeped in thought. What started as a fun sparring match had quickly turned into a revelation of the serious consequences of his...*what*? Desertion? Was that how Amanda viewed his absence for the past eight years? She'd spoken as if she'd been promised something—his soon return. Wasn't that what she'd implied?

Well, the mail goes both ways, doesn't it?

After the first year or so, she'd never contacted him again, either. No calls or texts. Nothing. Yet she had expected it from him. But why? People, *young* people, parted ways in the process of living and sometimes simply ended up going on separate paths.

He climbed into his BMW, turned the ignition, then headed back toward *Key News*. On the days leading up to his departure, she had become aloof, especially when he'd tried to discuss their future together. She'd told him she didn't want to hold him back—that the full scholarship was a gift he couldn't turn down. She'd baffled him. One minute they were planning their future, the next, she was pushing him away. He rubbed his fingers over his chin. Clearly, she'd forgotten her own role in his leaving.

At the time, he'd wondered what had gotten into her, pushing him to leave the way she had. He'd told her she was parroting his father's wishes. He'd found it infuriating, and now the memory of those wise, parental-sounding words seemed way out of character for the girl he used to know. Eventually, she'd worn him down and made him see the sense of it.

The day he'd left for college, she'd thrown her arms around his neck, and kissed him. *I'm expecting great things from you in the photojournalism world,* she'd said. *Just don't let that snooty eastern school change you.* Tears had filled her eyes then, too, but she'd brushed them away with her adorable smile and tear-glistened lashes. *I'll see you after the first semester,* he'd promised.

Except for a few short visits during his early college years, he never did come back. He'd loved it as much as she'd said he would.

She'd convinced him to go. And now she was...what...mad because he hadn't come back? That seemed petty and not like her at all.

He turned left on Market Street and drove one block to *Key News*, then parked in front of the building. As he walked up the short flight of steps to the entrance, he swore he'd get to the bottom of what ailed her. It was imperative they deal with the past, or they would never have a future together.

He cast a slight smile. He was still crazy about her, and if he handled things the right way, winning her back would be the fun part.

Ten minutes later, he sat at his large, oak office desk, sifting through his messages. As he did, he thought of an idea to spend more time with Amanda. He grabbed his cell phone and punched in Keller's number.

"Keller... Ethan Knight here," he said, with a quick check of the time on his watch—12:30. "I hope I'm not disturbing your lunch hour."

"Not at all. Good to hear from you, Ethan. What can I do for you?"

"I'd like to have Miss Marsh accompany me to the State Park to look over the facilities at the campground, especially where the girls are concerned. I'd feel more comfortable if a woman checked out the place in consideration of the female students and their needs."

"Splendid idea. I'll call her right away and let her know."

"Great. I'd like to leave tomorrow around eight a.m.," Ethan said.

"I'll have her call you this afternoon, and you two can work out the details."

"That's not necessary. Just tell her I'll text her where to meet."

"I'll call her right now."

Ethan punched end, giving Keller time to reach her first before sending his own text. He couldn't keep from smiling. She'd know he had a hand in this, and she'd be furious.

And tied to me for the entire day.

CHAPTER 9

Ethan held the passenger door open as Amanda marched across the parking lot to his vehicle. "Good morning," he said.

She stopped in front of him, eyes blazing, holding a Dunkin' Donut paper coffee cup. "This is my day to sleep in." She stomped her foot. "Mr. Keller all but ordered me to accompany you today."

"Sorry about that. I know it was last-minute, and when I talked to Keller yesterday, he suggested you," Ethan lied.

"And no sooner had he hung up, I get this..." She held up her iPhone. "...cryptic message."

You're to accompany me to Apalacha State Park.

School parking lot, Friday, 8:00 a.m.

He held her irate gaze with meaning. "You did say we were to keep all future communication between us, *short and to the point*, didn't you?"

The brief widening of her eyes was short-lived. She lifted her chin and pinned him with a frosty glare.

"Now, we can either continue to waste time standing by my car, or we can get on the road," Ethan said.

Their staring match continued as he held the door, until her chin lowered and her gaze faltered, signaling signs of surrender. Those actions may have indicated submission, but in no way did they represent her feelings on the subject. With a belligerent press of her lips, she all but threw herself into the seat.

Yup. This day is definitely going to be fun.

"I see you've learned to curb that temper of yours since we parted," he said as he got behind the wheel.

She grunted, held herself upright, and stared out the side window. He shook his head, pulled from the lot, and went north on Coleman Drive. In minutes, they passed the Green Parrot Bar and Grill, then Sonic, then turned north on County Highway 67.

They sat in silence for a good five minutes. He glanced right. She still hadn't moved from her earlier position. If the day secluded together among the soaring longleaf pines was to help move their relationship forward, he would get nowhere with her giving him the silent treatment. "Are you going to sit in the corner pouting like some twelve-year-old all the way to the park?"

She swung her head left. "You could have just called me yourself, instead of having Mr. Keller—"

"What, and have you refuse?" He shook his head. "I needed a woman to check out the facilities."

"I've already assigned Jenny Peterson to help you. She's the P.E. teacher and coaches the girls' volleyball team. She loves the outdoors and will be perfect as your assistant."

Ethan adjusted his hands on the steering wheel. "Since I'm teaching the course, I should get to choose my assistant."

"Look, I know you've graduated to the *world traveler level,* leaving us simple, small-town, fishing-village folk behind, but let me remind you...*this* is Apalacha Key and pickings are slim in the qualified female teacher's department."

She blew out a sigh and shook her head. "If Jenny doesn't suit you, there's always Margaret Simms."

"Any relation to Mike Simms?" he asked.

"They're fraternal twins. Margaret is just a capable as Jenny. She's young and full of energy and also loves the outdoors." Amanda let out a heartfelt-sounding sigh. "I'll tell you what. You can meet each of them, and then decide."

"Well, you're the one that's here now, so how about we focus on today and worry about my assistant tomorrow?"

"Fine."

"There's a thermos behind my seat if you'd like some more coffee. I could use another cup."

Amanda twisted in her seat and reached behind his. She grabbed his green thermos and placed it between her legs. "Is this the one—"

"You gave me? Yes."

She unscrewed the top and poured an ample amount into his Yeti mug.

"There you go." His fingers brushed along the back of her hand as he took it from her. He hadn't touched her since he'd returned, and the feel of her soft skin evoked sweet memories.

"Thank you." He lifted the mug and took a sip.

"It's held up rather well," she said.

"What?"

"The thermos."

"Oh, right," he said. "The Aladdin Stanley thermos is still one of the best as far as thermoses go."

She topped off her Dunkin' Donut cup, then screwed the cap back on the container.

"Do you remember when you gave that to me?" He nodded at the thermos, now setting near her feet.

"Early birthday, right before you went on a long camping trip. Or something like that. I remember I had a heck of a time finding one. There were several online, but none of them were in very good condition."

"Where did you eventually get it?"

"My dad."

"He found it for you?"

"Yep, in his garage."

"Whaaat?"

"It was his and in excellent condition, and since he seldom used it, he gave it to me to give to you."

"I didn't know that." He shot a quick glance at her profile. "Remember what you said when you gave it to me?"

She took a sip from her cup and lifted her left shoulder. "Something about it keeping you warm."

"You handed it to me and said, *to keep you warm until you come back to me.*"

She ran her finger along the lid of her cup.

"At the time, I thought that was very romantic," he said.

She nodded. "We had our share of romance. Young love and all that." Her flippant tone made light of it.

"And very sweet. *You* were very sweet."

"Yes, we had a history."

"I confess, during that four-day backpacking trip, I fell asleep each night dreaming of how you would keep me warm after I returned." He grinned.

"And that was then, and this is now," she said.

"Right."

* * *

Amanda breathed in deeply, making every effort to still her pounding heart. *Ethan would have to evoke sweet memories from our past and this early in the day, too.* It was only half-past nine, and she was already in an emotional tizzy.

She'd scoured antique malls and online stores for many days looking for that thermos. At seventeen, she'd already thought of him as her future husband. In her mind, she was already his wife. It had been so important for her to be the woman who took care of her man, even back then.

She'd worried about him trekking off in the dead of winter into the Appalachian Mountains on some four-day survival excursion. He'd assured her the park guide knew what he was doing, and therefore, no need for worry.

The coffee thermos had been her way of giving him both sustenance and warmth during his journey—a token of her desire to take care of him. Eyeing it now on the floorboard at her feet, it was still that and more. It also represented the memories of a young heart filled with love and the hope of a future with Ethan.

Those years are gone...lost...

"There's the park sign and the turnoff," Ethan said. "We're almost there."

Minutes later, they came to the red entrance sign embossed with the words, *Apalacha State Park*, in white lettering. Ethan turned off the black, asphalt highway onto a picturesque road of white sand, flanked on both sides with the soaring longleaf pine trees the park was known for.

Following the markers to the park ranger's office took another ten minutes. Ethan parked the car, and they got out and stretched their legs. The park ranger waved and walked toward them. He shook hands with Ethan and tipped his hat to her.

"Are you two the representatives from the high school who inquired about having an overnight event in three weeks?"

"Yes, I'm Ethan Knight, and this is Amanda Marsh. We'd like directions to Buckhorn Hunt campground."

"Easy, Buckhorn Hunt Primitive is in blue. Just follow the signs, look for the blue, and it'll lead you right to it."

"What did he mean by primitive?" Amanda asked, when they got back in the car. "We can't expect the girls to go without bathrooms or water."

"Don't worry, they won't. I made sure this campground has some amenities but also some *roughing it*. Let's just check it out and see, okay?"

"All right."

The car bumped along for about twenty more minutes until they came to Buckhorn. The campsite opened onto a large circle, surrounded by tall, longleaf pines. A few small, blooming magnolias nestled amongst soaring trees, trying their best to reach sunlight.

Ethan pulled to a stop. Hands still on the wheel, he leaned forward and looked through the windshield. They opened their respective doors and got out, both silently surveying the campground.

"You can't be serious?" Amanda said.

Ethan cut his eyes in her direction. "Let's take a look around before deciding on the verdict."

"The lake is pretty, and the pines offer great shade," she said. "That should at least help with the summer heat." She lifted her iPhone and took a few short recordings as well as stills of the area.

He nodded and walked toward a narrow shed-like structure left of the camp's center. "Is this what I think it is?"

"What?" Amanda followed behind and stopped next to

him. She snapped a couple of photos as he pulled the door open.

"It's a toilet," he said.

Amanda peered through the narrow opening and gasped. "You can't expect the girls to use that thing?"

"It's either that or a private spot in the woods—with a trowel and a roll of toilet paper."

"Absolutely not! I will not have my teenage girls subjected to that kind of humiliation. Buddy, you *have* been away too long. Do you have any idea what that would do to their self-esteem, especially with boys around? Boys they know. Boys some of the girls may have a crush on?"

He stared at her and said nothing as if her words sparked a memory. To her horror, his mouth quirked and his eyes grew openly amused. "I remember now," he finally said. "As I recall, you had one such experience."

Heat flooded into her cheeks. "You *would* bring that up."

"Oh, come on. It was cute."

"Is this why you wanted me to come with you today, to remind me of our past? First the thermos, and now the...the bathroom experience?"

"You mean the *trowel in the woods* experience?" The trace of laughter in his voice nearly undid her.

She stomped toward the car, stopped, then turned back to him. "The answer to this place is N.O. *No*. This workshop will not happen without a suitable campsite with his *and* her amenities, a firepit, electricity..." She ticked off each with her fingers. "...and a picnic table, to name a few."

He hustled after her. "That defeats the point of the survival aspects of the course." He caught up with her and grabbed her arm, stopping her midstride.

"You can teach survival skills without humiliating the

girls," she said. "If this were an all-male course, then that would be different."

He pulled a list from his jeans pocket and handed it to her. "There's another spot I'd planned to check out—Harper's Hunt. We'll take a look and see if it meets your satisfaction."

She blew out a breath and gave a curt nod. "Well, why didn't you say so?"

Before she could turn toward the car, he placed both of his hands on her upper arms and held her in front of him. "And I'm sorry the porta-potty back there brought up an unpleasant memory." The gleam of humor in his eyes said otherwise. "But you coming from the woods with toilet paper trailing all the way to the ground from somewhere underneath your shorts was rather funny to a bunch of teenage boys." His smile broadened. "Even now, I remember it was quite adorable."

She jerked out of his arms and stomped to the car, resisting the urge to cover her ears against his merry chuckle.

Chapter 10

Ethan walked around the second campsite, which was not near as picturesque as the first one, but it had slightly better amenities.

Amanda meandered around, taking videos and photos. "Well at least this site has *two* of those awful porta-potties."

"And one picnic table which won't be enough for ten or twelve people." Ethan stepped over to a metal post that stood about three feet in the air. "Here's your electricity."

She moved near him and snapped a photo. "We can bring a few extension cords, and maybe we could string up some lights between the trees."

"Or we can use lanterns and candles," he said. "Those and the light from a fire should be sufficient."

She stood, gazing around the site. "This one's better as far as basic conveniences, but I think the kids would love the lake."

He nodded and glanced around the area. "I think we should use the first spot."

She rounded on him, but he raised his hand before she could speak. "You may not realize this, but part of learning to survive in the wilderness is as much mental as physical. If we provide amenities, they will miss the mental exercise."

"This is a beginner course, Ethan. Why not let them take baby steps? Then...and I can't believe I'm going to say this...if they enjoy this one, we can offer a more advanced course using what they've learned, but in a more realistic situation."

"A nice idea, Mandy, but I don't know how long I'll be in town. I'd prefer to give them the entire experience the first go-around."

Her eyes widened a fraction, and she blinked. He'd clearly surprised her. "I thought you said you'd be here for the summer. The second course could be held two or three weeks after the first one."

"Is that a roundabout way of saying you'd like for me to stay?"

"Only for the students. If...if it helps them, then yes."

"Like I said, I don't fully know what my plans are, so I'd like to execute the course as planned and do it right."

A determined gleam entered her eyes. "I'm sorry, but I can't okay this part of the course if you insist on these primitive arrangements."

He folded his arms and focused on her haughty, high-school-principal glare he was quickly coming to loathe. "What if we let the kids decide? You've taken enough photos and videos of both places. Let's show them the pictures and give them the ugly details of each and let them chose which site. I've already reserved both, and we can have the students decide in time for me to cancel one of them. What do you say?"

She folded her arms, matching his. "What if it's fifty-fifty?"

"Then I'll let you be the deciding vote."

"All right. Fine." She nodded.

They headed out of the park, and Ethan felt he hadn't put so much as a dent into mending their relationship. Maybe a good meal would help his cause.

He slowed his BMW at the restaurant near the park exit. "You hungry?"

She met his gaze with a slight look of surprise. "I could eat something."

He turned the car into the parking lot and stopped. "I've heard their specialty is deep-fried catfish, caught fresh at the lakes here."

"Sounds good."

The hostess seated them at a booth near the window, and they both ordered the catfish special and iced tea.

Amanda retrieved a spiral notebook from her purse and opened it to a blank page. He noticed she'd also included a copy of his supplies list. She spread it open on the tabletop.

"Your list looks thorough," she said. "Let's see...you've got tents, lighting gear, matches, utensils..." Amanda stopped and sat back as the waitress set the iced tea in front of them. "Thanks."

"Thank you," Ethan said.

"My pleasure," the waitress replied. "Your meal will be out shortly." She collected the menus and left.

Amanda turned her focus back on the list. "You've covered everything, except food." She looked him in the eyes. "What were you thinking about? Are we catching our own fish, rummaging for berries and edible mushrooms?" Her tone dripped with sarcasm.

"Something like that, yes." He held her gaze.

"I can see you haven't spent much time around teenagers. Their appetites are off the chart, even the girls. How many fish are you hoping to catch, anyway? Believe me, it'll take a lot more than a few paltry trout to satisfy fifteen and sixteen-year-olds."

He opened his mouth to speak.

"And if we can't catch enough fish to feed ten hungry teenagers," Amanda rambled on, "then what?"

He waited a few seconds to make sure she was through. "Then we can have some extra food on hand in case we come up short. Believe me, the last thing I want is for the students to go hungry. That said, I'd like to keep that bit of info to ourselves. If they think they'll only eat what we catch or find, then they'll take the job more seriously."

She sat back and gave a curt nod. "I can live with that."

Ethan placed his elbows on the table, fisting his hands underneath his chin. Amanda tilted her head to one side and studied the sheet. As she did so, she lifted her hand and tucked a stray, tawny lock behind her left ear. She abruptly looked up as if suddenly aware of his scrutiny. For a moment, he thought she was going to say something. But she just licked her lips and blinked.

"Anything else you wish to discuss?" He nodded toward the paper in her hands.

She swallowed and shook her head. "You've listed all the usual stuff—seems you've thought of everything. A waterproof lighter—emergency blankets." She glanced at him. "You really think we'll need those with this heat?"

"Not likely, but it's better to have a few on hand in case of emergencies."

She commenced her perusal. "I see you've included a water purifier." She didn't need to say another word. Her appalled features said it all. "Is it your plan to drink the lake water?"

"That was the general idea, but we can also bring bottled water if that makes you feel better."

"It does, thank you. Let's see...you have lanterns, batteries, and sleeping pads." She grinned, and his heart all but stopped. She hadn't *really* smiled at him since he'd returned. Amanda had no idea what her smile did to him, and he wondered if she ever had. There was a time when her gorgeous smile could make him agree to just about anything she wanted.

"I'm surprised at the sleeping pads," she continued. "I figured you'd want them to experience total discomfort."

"They have to be blown up by mouth, so I'll leave it to them if they want to go to all that trouble." He removed the straw from its paper. "So, are you dating anyone?" He plunged the straw into the tea, then took a sip.

She lifted a finely plucked eyebrow. "I'm sure you're already aware of that answer."

"I've heard rumors, but I'd like to hear it from you."

"Yes, I'm dating someone."

"So. Who is this special man in your life?"

"Daryl Cleveland."

He frowned, trying to recall the name. "Not the heavyset kid who blew up the chemistry lab?"

"That's the one."

He threw back his head and laughed. "*Daryl, the barrel, Cleveland*? Are you serious?"

"And just what is wrong with Daryl?"

"Nothing if you like a barrel-sized, boring, uninteresting, walking disaster zone—"

"Daryl has changed a lot from the high school boy you and I used to know. He's lost weight, he's kind, thoughtful, competent, and he's dependable."

"And quite vanilla, I'm sure."

"I happen to like vanilla."

"No, you don't. You like cherry cream cheese. That's your go-to flavor, not vanilla."

"And how about you? Dating anyone in particular?"

He shook his head. "Not at the moment."

"Not even Miss *Clingy*?"

He gaped at her in confusion. "Who?"

"Miss, *poured into a black dress*, Adele? Posing in at least a dozen pictures with you over the years."

"Ah, yes... Adele Van Dorn. Dutch and as I recall, *very* fond of tulips." He smiled as he recalled an especially nice moment, but quickly stifled it at Amanda's sour expression.

"Can we please change the subject?" she said. "I have no interest in discussing Daryl or Adele with you any further." She folded the paper and stuffed it—along with her notebook—into her purse just as the waitress placed their catfish in front of them.

"Mmm, this looks great," she said and dug in.

He eyed her for a moment. "I see you still eat like a field hand." He just couldn't resist saying it.

She paused, fork midair, and glared at him.

"Don't get me wrong, I like a woman with an appetite." He smothered a grin at her vexed expression.

"You know darn well I burned a lot of calories during my cheerleading years."

"Ah yes, all those summersaults in that little short skirt."

She lowered her knife and fork and surveyed him with what he'd come to know as her schoolmarm stare. "Are you done?"

"Yes, ma'am." He grinned.

They spent the rest of the meal in companionable silence. After Ethan polished off the last morsel, he glanced at his watch. "I think it's time we got back."

She dabbed her mouth with a napkin and nodded. "This

was delicious. Thank you for dinner. Maybe we can treat the students to a meal here after the campout. Since you're paying for almost everything else, I'm sure the school budget can afford it." She picked up her purse and edged toward the end of the seat.

He stood aside while she slid from the booth. "Especially if they have to survive on wild berries, mushrooms, and a few paltry fish," he said.

Her eyes held a definitive twinkle. "Exactly."

* * *

The drive back to Apalacha Key didn't seem to take as long. Maybe having had the ice broken—as far as their relationship went—and her stomach full, made the difference.

Amanda unlocked her Mini Cooper and waved goodbye in response to Ethan's farewell salute. Once in her car, she sent a short text to Annie.

Back home.

Looking forward to tomorrow's LNO session.

See you at nine.

Amanda passed by the beach on her way home, and since it was still daylight, she decided to go for a swim and an evening stroll. She pushed through the side door of her little blue-and-white bungalow and quickly changed into her sunburst-orange bikini. She slipped a coral-and-aqua coverup over her head and left.

People of all shapes and sizes dotted the white sand with their colorful beach chairs arranged side by side, facing west. Since the sun set around 7:30 p.m., it offered plenty of daylight for a quick swim before her stroll.

White foam covered her ankles, lifting and dancing to her

shins as she waded into the Gulf of Mexico. Once hip deep, she threw her body forward. With long, even strokes, she slid into the blue-green water, reveling in the smooth, salty warmth. A swift turn had her floating on her back, offering the view of slow-moving clouds overhead.

Just what she needed after spending seven hours with Ethan Knight. Spending the day managing her emotions had been exhausting. He'd complimented her on controlling her outbursts. *Ha!* If he could have only heard what went on in her head.

Ready for her walk, she pulled herself upright, tread water for a moment, then swam for the shore. In minutes, she was fighting the pull of surf on her ankles. Breaking free of its tug, she stood to her feet, sprinted the last few steps to her coverup, and slipped it overhead as she began her walk.

Families and couples had gathered and were now seated in their chairs, sipping wine, ready for nature's big show. She stopped to watch as well. This act of nature held a ceremonial feel, and she never tired of the sight, but it always surprised her how people clapped when the sun finally melted beyond the horizon.

She continued her walk and spotted Ethan coming toward her. She hesitated and glanced back at her parked car. Should she try and make a run for it? When she looked back, he lifted his hand and smiled. *Oh, bother.* Should she stand there and wait, or walk toward him? Or better still, should she pretend she hadn't seen him and amble back to her car?

She groaned. She did not want to engage him. *You're an adult, Amanda, so act like it.*

"Hello." She forced a smile as he neared her.

"Hi." He stopped in front of her. "I see you're out for an end-of-day stroll. Mind if I join you?"

"Actually, I was just about to go back home."

"Good, I'll come with you."

"What?"

"I'd like to talk with you about something."

"We've talked all day. Can't it wait?"

"I'd rather it didn't." He took her arm and led her to her car. "I'll hitch a ride with you, if that's okay."

"Why can't you come in your own car?"

He waved his arm back over his shoulder as he walked her forward. "Oh, it's parked way down at the other end of the boulevard."

"Okay. Fine—since you don't seem to be giving me much choice in the matter."

They got to her Mini Cooper, and she opened the door on the driver's side.

"You don't lock your car?" Ethan lifted an enquiring brow.

"That's not necessary here."

He waited until she took her seat, then walked around to the passenger side and got in. "I bet Sheriff Hawke would have something to say about that attitude."

She inserted her key and started the ignition. "So, you two are now buddy-buddy?"

"Why not? I've made amends, and both he and Annie have accepted my apology."

"Good for you." She turned right out of the parking area, then took an immediate left toward her house.

"Don't tell me you're still holding a grudge on their behalf?"

"And if I am?"

"Withholding forgiveness will only hurt *you* in the long run."

"How philosophical." She parked in front of her house

and watched him unfold his frame from her car. She quickly joined him, and they walked to her side door. She turned the handle and stepped inside, leaving him to follow.

"I see you don't lock your house, either."

She spun around to face him. "Look, I have things to do, so what do you want to talk to me about?"

"What things?"

"I have plans to take a stress-relieving bath, followed by two aspirins and an early night."

"Can we eat something first?"

"You can't be hungry after our late lunch."

"Speak for yourself. Besides, that was four hours ago." He stepped around her and headed for the kitchen.

She threw up her hands. "By all means, come right on in. I'm sure you can find everything you need, since nothing has changed since you were last here."

"I wouldn't say, *nothing*...I see you got rid of that ugly, pea-green sofa your dad bought."

She followed him to the kitchen and plopped into the nearest kitchen chair. "You can make your own sandwich."

"Who says I want a sandwich?"

"Because there's very little else to eat."

He yanked open the fridge door and assessed the contents. "Is this all you've got?"

"Yes. This happens to me my day to go to the grocery store." She smiled sweetly.

He pulled out the makings for a hearty sandwich—sliced ham, Swiss cheese, a tomato, lettuce, bread-and-butter pickles, and some condiments. He spun toward her. "Where's the bread?"

She rested her cheek in her palm. "Oh gee, I'm all out. I'd planned to buy more today."

"Why didn't you say something before I pulled out all this stuff?"

She could hardly stop the merriment she felt at that moment, but when he started to pile the ingredients onto a plate, she stood. "Hold on, a minute." She stepped over to the fridge and pulled a frozen loaf from the freezer. "Here." She handed him the bread. "You'll have to toast it."

She took her seat and watched him unwrap the whole-wheat loaf. Physically, he was still quite something, but for the life of her, she didn't understand why he seemed intent on her company. Unless...unless, he had a renewed interest in her. Her heart caught in her throat. *What if he did?* She swallowed and pushed that crazy thought out of her head.

"Do you have anything more on the website about my survival course?" He retrieved the toasted bread and tossed it on his plate. "Last time I checked, it was pretty sketchy."

"Not yet." She stood and crossed over to the fridge. "I was waiting to have your completed syllabus with the course description and info about the campsite before I posted any more."

"That's a good place to make very clear what this workshop's about." He slathered mustard on a warm slice of bread. "If we need to have a meeting with the parents, we can do that, too, and then the kids can decide which campsite they prefer."

She poured them each a glass of iced tea, set one at his place, then sat back down. "Why don't you write up the course description to your satisfaction, and I'll have Sally post it on the website?"

"I'll get that to you on Monday when I bring in the syllabus and description." He finished stacking the toast with the ingredients from the fridge. "You got any chips?" He bit into the sandwich.

"Sure." She once again pushed her body from the chair with exaggerated effort, found a bag in the cabinet next to the microwave, and held it out to him. "Sea salt all right with you?"

"Mmmm, my favorite. Thanks."

She sat back down, took a sip of tea, then made a deliberate action of looking at her watch. "Now that we've taken care of your appetite, was there anything else besides the website you wished to discuss?"

Eyeing her, he took a swig of his tea and nodded. "Us."

"Us?"

"More specifically this thing between us."

"There is no *thing* between us, hasn't been for a long time."

"Don't play dumb. You know what I'm talking about—your *avoidance* thing." He took another bite of his ham-and-Swiss, chewed with purpose, then swallowed. "We're going to be working together in some capacity whether you like it or not. And since the day I've returned, you've done everything in your power to evade, circumvent, or sidestep me."

"Oh, I don't know." She sat back and crossed her legs. "So far, I think my tactics are working quite well." She took another swig of tea. "I see no need to change them." She snapped up one of his sweet pickle slices and popped it in her mouth. "Once I get you settled with Jenny, the less involved I'll be, too."

"I don't want her as my assistant. I want you."

She sucked in a controlling breath. "You'll have Jenny, and you'll like it," she said through clenched teeth.

"Why can't I have *your* help?"

"Because I'm the school principal. I—I have other responsibilities."

"Like what?"

She rolled her eyes. "Like overseeing the other summer courses. In one way or another, I'm pretty much involved in all of them."

"Then assign this Miss Peterson to handle those, and you can help me."

"If this is your way of trying to wear me down, it won't work. I'm over you, Ethan." She stood and made her way to the door. "Now, if you'll excuse me, it's been a long day."

He stood, set his plate in the sink, and followed. "Can I at least help with the dishes before I go?"

"Out!"

Amanda did not miss the light of amusement in Ethan's eyes as he stepped onto the front porch. She slammed the door behind him. "Infuriating, aggravating man."

She stomped back to the kitchen and yanked open the freezer door. "Please be here." She rummaged underneath the frozen items, tossing aside packages of meat and bags of berries. "Yes!" There, in the bottom, underneath a box of frozen spinach sat a small carton of cherry cream cheese ice cream.

After grabbing a spoon, she carried it and the sweet cream into her living room. She curled up on one end of the sofa, peeled off the lid, and dug in. The instant the cherry goodness touched her lips, she gave a heavenly sigh. She determined then and there to stock up on the creamy dessert. If the rest of the summer turned out like that day's events, she'd need a freezer full.

Chapter 11

Saturday, Amanda met Annie at LNO's office bright and early, carrying a box of assorted muffins. She turned on the lights and made her way to the break room to start the coffee.

"Good morning, Mandy." Annie waltzed in, bubbling with excitement, and tossed her purse on the desk. She wore slim-fitting jeans, white sneakers, and an off-the-shoulder blouse in a tiny, multi-colored floral.

"Good morning, yourself. Love that blouse."

"Isn't it adorable?" She reached into her purse and pulled out a stack of yellow envelopes. "It's one of Jill Jeffrey's designs for summer."

"What do you have there?" Amanda asked.

"Mae Miles Salon donated gift certificates for a half-hour manicure." She handed the stack to Amanda. "Here... Just slide one in the front pocket of each backpack."

They entered the conference room, and Amanda began placing the gift envelopes in each pack. "You're still expecting eight girls, right?"

"That's right. They're between the ages of fifteen and sixteen."

Together, they placed the cheery backpacks at each seat, along with the LNO workbook and sparkly pen.

Annie made one more walk-around, making a few adjustments to the presentation. "Several of the students are on family vacation and were disappointed to miss today, but I promised to have several more sessions before school starts."

Amanda checked her watch. "We have thirty minutes before they arrive. I've made coffee and brought muffins."

"Perfect, I could use another cup." Annie looped her arm through Amanda's. "And I want an update on your outing with Ethan."

Settled in the break room, they took a moment to relax and enjoy their coffee.

"Before you take another bite of that muffin," Annie said, "I want details."

Amanda had just popped a bit of blueberry muffin into her mouth and wanted to savor the moist cake-like confection. She shot her friend the evil eye and was rewarded with Annie's wide grin.

Amanda took her time swallowing, then slowly sipped her coffee. "Nothing much to tell. We drove to the park, checked out a couple of campsites, and then stopped for a late lunch before driving back."

"Okay, but what did you find to talk about in the *in-between* moments?" She cradled her coffee mug in her hands, eyeing Amanda with giddy anticipation.

"As you would expect, there was the usual sparring—"

"Oh, that's good."

"What do you mean, good?"

"It means, good sexual tension." Annie's eyes filled with

merriment. "It's what makes a relationship exciting." She sipped from her mug. "Keep going."

Amanda shook her head with mock surrender. "And then there were his irritating referrals to our past—"

"That sounds really interesting. Good or bad?"

"Both, actually."

"And the sparring, what was that about?" Annie broke off a piece of muffin.

"The facilities." Amanda scrunched up her face and shivered. "Oh Annie, you should see where he plans to take the kids. Both sites we looked at are for primitive camping, and they have the absolute worst possible conditions. I shudder to think what the girls will do."

"Will you nix the course, then?"

Amanda groaned. "I don't think I can. Mr. Keller is so keen on it."

"From your description of the campsites, I certainly wouldn't like that part of it."

"We've come up with *some* semblance of a compromise." She stood and tossed the dregs of her coffee into the small sink. "But even with that, I don't see how the girls will enjoy it."

"Maybe they're tougher than you think." Annie followed Amanda to the sink.

The teens started arriving a few minutes before ten. Their sparkling chatter as they entered the building alerted Amanda and Annie to their presence.

Annie leaned toward Amanda. "To be continued." She winked and headed to the conference room.

They exchanged greetings as each girl took their place at the long table.

Amanda moved to the entrance and waited until Annie

began to teach the class. She had a rare ability to communicate with humor, excitement, and joy. No wonder the girls gave her their full, undivided attention. Annie had a gift that stemmed from a loving, caring heart for the teens.

Amanda knew a little of Annie's story—about the emotional abuse she'd suffered from her father. Maybe that was what gave her friend such an edge with the young ladies. Annie's compassion encircled every word she spoke.

"Now," Annie said, "before we get into the first session, let's have some real fun." She placed her palms together and grinned. "Ladies, open your backpacks."

Amanda left to man the desk while Annie held court in the conference room amid the girly, squeals of delight.

* * *

Monday morning, Ethan arrived with the documents Amanda had requested. He signed in at the school's front desk, then made his way to her office.

Unlike his previous visits, he found her desk cluttered and crowded with stacks of files and papers marked with sticky notes. She stood in front of an open file drawer, running her fingers over the tabs. She stopped to insert a manila folder. He watched her from the doorway. When she shoved the drawer closed, he tapped on the doorframe, alerting her to his presence.

She spun around and frowned, then glanced at the wall clock. "I wasn't expecting you for another twenty minutes."

"I finished earlier at the paper than I thought I would." He surveyed the array of stacked paper products. "But it looks like I should have waited."

She motioned for him to take a seat, while pushing the

mass of folders and files to one side. "Just doing a bit of organizing now that the halls are quiet." She settled back into her chair. "How are things going at the paper? You don't seem to work that many hours there?"

"That's because I don't. Ned Baker has been running the place for over a year since my dad died. As far as I can tell, he's got everything under control. Except for the occasional question, I'm not needed much at all."

She pushed a strand of her nut-brown hair behind her right ear. "You're a journalist. I'm surprised you don't have any more interest than that?"

"According to you, I *used* to be a journalist."

"You still could be." She fidgeted with the cuff of her sleeve. "You own a newspaper. You could turn it into something really special for you and the town—bring it up to date yourself."

"Right now, my time is consumed by my freelance work and *Knight Owl*."

"Oh." She gnawed her lower lip for a moment, then leaned forward. A sudden sparkle glimmered in her eyes. "What if you incorporated that *Owl* thing into *Key News*? Made it a weekly part, or daily if you wanted." She sat back. "Of course, you'd have to add...much better content to it."

"Be careful, or I might think you want me to stay."

His eyes met hers, and a flush crept up her cheeks. Her dark eyelashes fluttered as she briefly lowered her gaze.

She roughly cleared her throat. "My main concern is for those working at the paper and to keep our news controlled by locals, not by some conglomerate out of New York or Atlanta. That should be yours, too. You can go online or to any grocery store and buy national papers. I think it's a shame to lose the local element that your paper brings and has always brought to this town for almost four generations."

"Now you're sounding like my grandmother."

She spread her hands before him. "She's a wise woman."

"She is...on occasion."

The earnest expression on Amanda's pretty face truly touched him. She really wanted to save him. He hated to disappoint her, as this was the first friendly move from her to what...*reconcile*?

He shook his head. "I'm afraid that just doesn't interest me right now."

"Just *Knight Owl*."

"That's correct."

She clasped her hands on top of the desk, studying him. "What is so special about that rag? I've read it, and I'm sad to say I would never pay for it. I mean, who would? It doesn't seem to have any meaningful substance."

"Then why do you persist in worrying about it?"

"Because that dribble takes no talent." She slowly shook her head. "Why would you set aside all you've accomplished for that?"

"It's none of your business."

"Like hell it's not. I gave up—" Amanda sucked in air, and her luminous eyes widened in shock.

"Gave up what?"

"Nothing. I—I don't know why I said that." Her head jerked right to left. "I guess I just feel invested in you." She snatched up a pencil and began rolling it between her fingers. "I know how gifted you are, and I hate to see you throw away everything you've worked for." Her gaze fell. She tossed the pencil aside and gathered up the papers on her desk. "M—Must be the teacher in me. I hate to see talent go to waste."

What was she about to say? He gnawed the inside of his lip. What was she hiding from him?

"I'm sorry, Ethan. It's your life. You certainly don't need my input." Amanda pressed her lips tightly together and shuffled the papers into a neat stack. "You have every right to sell out, and no one should try to convince you otherwise."

"Thank you," he said, unable to stem the sarcasm. "However, my plans are not to *sell out* but to find a good match for my paper and my employees. And only if everything meets to my satisfaction."

"And have you found that...satisfactory buyer yet?" Her chest heaved, but she spoke calmly and with some effort, obviously in her attempt at handling her emotions.

Following her cue, he shook his head. "Just starting the process. I have an excellent newspaper broker managing the search."

"I see." She refolded her hands and glanced at the packet in his hand. "Is that for me?"

"As requested." He tossed the envelope on top of her desk."

She opened it and made a quick perusal of the contents. "Excellent."

"You've barely looked at it."

"I'm sure it's fine." Her hands shook as she pressed the intercom button on her desk phone. "Sally, I have the survival course info ready for the website."

"Be right there, Miss Marsh."

A moment later, Sally entered the office. "Hello," she said, and her bright smile encompassed both of them.

"Hi," Ethan said.

"Here you go, Sally." Amanda handed her the course description.

"Thanks." She smiled again and left.

"That's my cue to leave." Ethan stood and nodded at the

syllabus in her hands. "If you have any questions, I'm only a phone call away."

Amanda stood, too. "Of course. Thank you. Um, I guess we'll wait to see if any of the parents have any questions about the workshop." She fingered the chain around her neck. "And the um, primitive nature of the campsites."

He just watched her for a moment. It seemed she was doing her best to hold onto her composure. "I guess we will," he said.

"Until, then..." She cleared her throat. "If you need anything else as you prepare, just holler."

"I will." He walked to the door. "Be seeing you."

Ethan had taken about six steps before something compelled him to turn around. Amanda sat, slumped at her desk, with her face in her hands. He fought the desire to go back into her office and have it out with her once and for all. Her words and reactions to them confirmed his suspicion that something had happened all those years ago. Her assumption that he'd given up journalism for *Knight Owl* was somehow wrapped up in all of it. She was clearly upset, and he wished he understood why. But now was not the time to confront her. Not here at the school. He'd let it sit for the time being.

Once outside, he strode to his car, clicked the open button on his key fob, and climbed in. He and his grandmother were due for another conversation. She knew something—he was certain of it.

Still, as he drove back to the newspaper, none of that could erase the vision of Amanda's stunned, pallid face.

What were you about to say, Amanda? What did you give up?

CHAPTER 12

Tuesday morning at the school had been uneventful. Amanda decided to check the two online workshops due to start the following Monday. Happy to see Mike's course had met more than the ten required, she then clicked on Ethan's. So far, two had signed up; not surprising as the info had only gone up the day before.

She glanced at her watch and noted it was time to meet Daryl for lunch. She turned off her laptop and headed out. A few minutes later, she pushed through the doors at Dairy Delight.

"Amanda."

She turned to see Ethan's grandmother sitting in the booth by the entrance. "Hey, Miss Ida." Amanda stopped to greet the elderly lady. "You by yourself?"

"For the moment. Ethan is joining me for lunch in a bit." Miss Ida adjusted her eyewear. "Won't you sit down until he comes?"

That was the last thing Amanda wanted to do, especially after the previous morning's meeting with him. She glanced at the counter, then back to Miss Ida. "Sure, but only for a minute. I don't have much time. I'm meeting a friend for a quick bite, then I have to go right back to the school."

She slid onto the red and white vinyl bench across from Miss Ida, smiling as she did so.

"How are you, Amanda?" Miss Ida asked. "I've been thinking a lot about you lately."

With Ethan back in town, it wasn't hard to understand Miss Ida's meaning. "All good thoughts, I hope," she said, not quite sure how else to respond.

Miss Ida gazed at her and smiled. "Always, dear." She scooted forward. "Ethan says he's working with you on a school project right now."

"That's right." Amanda nodded. "He's going to be leading one of our summer workshops for the students."

"Amanda..."

Here it comes.

"Since you're short on time, I'll come right to the point." Miss Ida laced her fingers together and placed her hands on the table. "Ethan is suspicious about something you said the day he left for school. And I need to tell you... I know what my son said to you."

Amanda swallowed. So, Miss Ida knew? Amanda struggled internally, not quite sure what to say to that news. She shot a quick glance at the entrance. *Where are you, Daryl?* "I'd rather not go there, Miss Ida. What's in the past is past. And if that's all—"

"I feel terrible about what Jim said, and I can't imagine what that must have done to you, honey."

"Like I said, it's all water under the bridge. Nothing can be done about it now except go forward, as both Ethan and I have been doing."

"But he's suspicious. I don't know how long I can keep the truth from him."

"Why tell him now when you've known all this time?"

"I didn't know anything until Jim told me on his deathbed." Her eyes filled with anxiety and concern. She lifted her hands, pleading for Amanda to understand. "I think you should tell Ethan what his dad said to you. Ethan should know. Even though I only know the gist of what Jim said, I've almost told Ethan myself, but I believe it's your place to do so."

"I don't agree," Amanda said. "Ethan knowing would only put Mr. Knight in a further bad light. I don't feel right about doing that. Besides, I *agreed* with the man. I agreed with the man Ethan despised. How do you think that will make me look in Ethan's eyes? Ethan told me that he and his father didn't have a good relationship. I don't know what happened between them, and I don't wish to know."

Amanda slipped from the booth. "I'm sorry, but I have to go." She turned and careened into Ethan's broad chest. His hands caught her arms, steadying her.

"Ethan." Amanda blinked and stared into his face, searching for any sign that he may have heard what she and his grandmother had been talking about. He must not have been standing there too long, or else Miss Ida would have said something.

Ethan glanced at his grandmother, then back at Amanda. "Don't leave on my account. Why don't you join us for lunch?"

"Thank you, but I'm meeting someone."

He dropped his hands from her arms. She rapidly sidestepped him and hurried away.

* * *

Ethan watched Amanda hustle over to the counter. He searched his grandmother's face as he took the seat Amanda had just vacated. "What was that all about?"

His grandmother peeked at him from under her lashes. "Just a visit between friends. She came in and when she saw me sitting here, I invited her to visit for a few minutes."

"By the look on Amanda's face you two must have been discussing something unsettling."

His grandmother lifted her napkin from the table, flicked it open, and laid it across her lap. At that moment, the waitress approached the booth.

"Good afternoon. What can I get you two?"

Ethan looked across the booth. "The usual, Grandma?"

She nodded and he turned toward the waitress. "We'll both have the daily special and iced tea, one sweet and one unsweet."

"Got it. I'll get those drinks right out."

He leaned forward and focused on his grandmother, giving her a look that clearly said he was done with playing games. "Now. What were you talking about that has Amanda darting away as if a Doberman was on her heels?"

"She was in a hurry when she got here, so I'm sure her *darting away* had nothing to do with you, dear."

He raised a brow and penned her with a silent look. "And you talked about...?"

"We talked a little bit about how things were going at the school."

"And that topic had her running away?"

She pressed her lips together. "Don't you use that sarcastic tongue with me."

"Then don't talk nonsense with *me*." He opened his napkin and laid it across his lap.

"It was simply a transition to what I really wanted to ask."

"Now we're getting somewhere." He sat back and folded his arms. "Which was...?"

"How you two were enjoying working together, or something of that nature."

"I can only imagine her response."

His grandmother adjusted her eyeglasses and cleared her throat. "She said you'd be leading one of the school's summer sessions."

"And that's what had her bolting?"

She smiled sweetly and shrugged as if she had no earthly idea why. She sighed and pressed a palm to her heart as the waitress returned with their iced tea and blue-plate special. How was it that the two most important women in his life could continue to blatantly evade his questions?

His grandmother forked a small amount of creamed potatoes and glanced up. "What are you thinking, Ethan?"

"Changing the subject?" He lifted a brow.

"As a matter of fact, I am." She gave him a long-leveled look.

He shook his head. "I'm thinking that one of these days you will tell me the truth, but right now, my country-fried steak is getting cold." He sliced the steak with his knife, jabbed a small piece with this fork, and shoved it into his mouth.

"You'll get indigestion eating like that."

Ethan scowled and kept eating.

"I can tell you still care for her." His grandmother's lips formed a gentle smile.

He swallowed, wiped his mouth with the napkin, and eyed her. "So what if I do?" He glanced over at the counter. At that moment, Amanda stood on tiptoe and placed a kiss on Daryl's cheek. *So that's who she was meeting.*

"He's taller than I remember," Ethan said, turning back to his grandmother. "What do you suggest I do? What sage advice do you have?" His questions rang with sarcasm.

"If you love her," she kindly said, apparently choosing to ignore his sarcasm this time, "you'll find a way to let her know. My advice is, deal with the past and your happily-ever-after will follow."

"So, you admit it? There *is* something about the past I need to address?"

"That's something for you and Amanda to work out." She reached across the table and grabbed his hand. "Talk with her, tell her how you feel, that you want to move forward *with* her." She released his hand. "That is, if you really want to."

Of course, he wanted to. In fact, his only thought was how to break up Daryl and Amanda. He took a swig of tea, cut another piece of steak, and shoved it between his lips.

"In my day, it was the man who did the chasing—the man who did the hunting," his grandmother said. "You're a hunter, aren't you? Why not apply some of that knowledge in this case?"

"Go after her, you mean?"

"Exactly."

He leaned toward his grandmother. "Well, for your information, that's exactly what I've been doing since I got back here."

He glanced over his shoulder and watched Amanda. She and Daryl sat with heads close together, smiling—talking.

"And how is that going?" she asked.

"She's fighting me every step of the way," he said without taking his eyes off Amanda. A thought struck him, and he lifted a finger. "I'll be right back." He slid from his seat and made his way to the counter, stopping inches from Amanda and Daryl.

"Daryl Cleveland, is that you?"

He turned and looked blankly at Ethan.

"It's Ethan. Ethan Knight." Daryl stared at him, dumfounded. "From high school," Ethan continued. "You and I were in the same chemistry class."

"Oh, right. I remember now," Daryl said. "How are you?"

They shook hands. "I'm doing well, thank you."

Ethan flashed Amanda with his most innocent expression. "Nice seeing you, too, Amanda."

"And you." Teeth clenched; she sent him a silent scowl.

He looked pointedly at the counter in front of them. "Having lunch?"

"Amanda is," Daryl said, "but I'm having dessert... Ahhh, here it comes."

The waitress set a bowl of vanilla ice cream at his place, and Daryl leaned back as if he were being presented with a feast.

"I see you like vanilla." Ethan glanced at Amanda who sat with her lips pressed together, holding in all matter of insults, he was certain.

"Good choice, fits you to a T."

Daryl's forehead creased in confusion as Ethan clamped his hand on the man's shoulder. "I'd better get back to my grandmother. I just wanted to say hi. Enjoy, you two."

His grandmother had barely finished her meal when she picked up her purse to leave.

"Where are you going?" he asked.

"Making myself scarce. I don't know what you said to Amanda, but by the look on her face she has something to say to you, and I get the feeling I shouldn't be privy to it." She slid from the booth and stood.

He glanced beyond her and noticed Daryl was also leaving.

"Thank you for lunch, sweetheart," his grandmother said. "I'll see you at dinner."

She left just as Amanda marched toward his table. To say she was put out with him was an understatement. She stopped in front of him, hoisting the strap of her purse snugly over her right shoulder. Cheeks flushed—her tawny eyes burned with emotion.

God she's adorable. "You are so cute when you're angry," he said.

"Are you *trying* to make my life miserable?"

"Because I came over to introduce myself to your boyfriend?"

"Is that what you call it?" she hissed. "You deliberately tried to humiliate him with that vanilla ice cream remark."

"Actually, I was trying to infuriate *you*. I've obviously succeeded." He grinned. "And if Daryl is slightly humiliated in the process..." He shrugged.

"In the future, kindly stay away from Daryl and me."

"Now...that's not very polite of you," Ethan said.

"I may have to tolerate your presence while you're employed by the school, but that's as far as it goes." She sharply inhaled. "You're playing some sort of game here, Ethan, and I don't like it. Stay out of my way, and I'll stay out of yours. Do you understand?"

"Oh, I understand all right, the prodigal has returned and messed up your carefully ordered, dull, and predictable little world. And as for staying out of your way, that'll be quite difficult in a town this size, so unless you want to spend your time at home for the duration of the summer, I'd suggest you get used to running into me."

"It may be inevitable to run into you, but I don't plan on getting used to it."

Chapter 13

Later that afternoon, Ethan listened to the newspaper staff as they discussed the next day's headlines. For the past ten to fifteen years, the small robust paper had slowly declined in sales. Despite the onset of the Internet and subsequent social media outlets taking over as consumers' first choice for newsgathering, Ethan's father had refused to join the digital world.

"I've got several items of interest for my Sunshine League column," Jeanne said, referring to her list. "One in hospital, two engagements, one birth announcement, and two deaths."

"I've got the ten-day forecast up and ready to go," Kayla jumped in with her information. "I've also got one more opinion piece to edit."

As Ethan listened, it became clear he needed to break in and manage the direction of the conversation. Their old-school methods weren't all bad but desperately needed updating, especially if there was any chance of saving and expanding the paper's reach, which hopefully would lead to the right buyer.

"Real estate listings are up." Patrick smiled with a glance around the room.

"A good sign Apalacha Key is growing," Ned added, eyeing Ethan. "Growth means future subscribers."

"And advertisers," Patrick added, with a hopeful expression.

"True, but that doesn't help with sales now." At Ethan's words, any sign of eagerness on the staff's part disappeared. "But that doesn't mean change can't take place," he amended, noticing their somber expressions. "So. What other stories do we have for tomorrow?"

"I've got an article on the current economic outlook of the country," Ned said.

The meeting went on like that for twenty more minutes. Obviously, those men and women loved what they did and believed their work was essential to the community.

He continued to listen to their discussion and input and felt the stirrings of a different sort. Amanda had accused him of *selling out,* and the more he thought about it, he could see why it looked exactly like that to the others. During that meeting, he found himself wanting to do more than sell out and leave. Several in that newsroom had been with *Key News* for decades, and half of them would be fired if he sold out. Didn't they deserve more than that?

* * *

Thursday morning, Amanda balanced a large box of donuts on one arm and pulled open the heavy glass door at the school's entrance with her other. She waved to Sally and made her way to a small room the school used as a large storage closet and flicked on the lights.

It housed a bank of shelving along one wall, an old student's desk and a low table in the center. She ran her gaze over the small space, making sure it had ample room for Ethan's deliveries. There were already two boxes in the far-left corner that had arrived the day before, and she assumed more would be coming in that day.

She'd alerted him the previous night via text that the boxes had arrived. His only response had been a thumbs-up emoji. He still kept their correspondence simple and to the point. *Good*. That worked for her. After his encounter and juvenile mocking of Daryl, the less she had to say to him, the better.

Satisfied, she walked down the hall to the teacher's lounge. She put the donuts on the counter and set about making a fresh pot of coffee.

Daryl aside, she still smarted from Ethan's other vile comments...*ordered, boring, and predictable,* he'd said. As the aroma of a fresh brew filled the room, she wondered if he was right. Had her life gotten so mundane that the operative words for her current state was dull and predictable?

Okay, she could understand the predictable part. Her job alone left her with few surprises, as most days ran along as expected. But boring? *No*. Working alongside high school students and their instructors was anything but dull.

The light on the coffee pot blinked *ready,* and she poured herself a mug. She turned from the coffee maker and froze. Ethan stood in the doorway—one shoulder against the doorjamb—quite openly studying her. She blinked and licked her lips. "You should've told me you were coming in this morning. I would've met you at the front office."

"I smelled the coffee and thought I'd grab a cup, if that's all right with you." He crossed over to the counter, not waiting for her reply.

"Help yourself." Amanda stepped aside. "The mugs are in the upper cabinet."

Ethan opened the cabinet door and selected a blue mug. "You're not still burned up about Daryl, are you?"

"Not in the least. Daryl's a big boy and can take care of himself. As to your behavior... I'm used to dealing with the antics of adolescent boys, and your conduct was no different."

Ethan threw back his head and laughed, and Amanda rolled her eyes. After he filled his cup, he joined her in the hallway, where they made their way to the closet room.

"Boxes are over there at the corner." She motioned with a tilt of her head.

He pulled a Swiss Army knife from his pocket and cut through the packing tape. He pushed the flaps aside, set the box to the right of the one underneath, then proceeded to open the second.

Amanda stepped across the room and peered inside the box nearest her. It held a packet of small flashlights, and another one had lighters.

She picked up one of the flashlights and balanced it in her hand. "These feel heavy-duty."

"They're tactical flashlights."

"Nice." She reached inside and pulled out another larger box, then opened the lid. It housed small emergency kits inside. "Where did you get these? Were they donated?"

"Yup. My grandmother has a contact at the hospital, and he ordered those for the kids."

"Do you mind if I open one?" she asked.

"Go ahead. I'm curious to see what's inside as well."

The emergency kits were small, red zippered packets that housed antibiotic cream, bandages, scissors, alcohol wipes, and what looked like individual packets of ibuprofen. "I don't see how this could come in handy if someone *really* got hurt," she said.

"It's only a basic kit. I'm planning to demonstrate more in-depth first-aid practices at the campsite. These small items are more symbolic than anything else. That said, the kits are perfect for minor cuts and issues, like a headache." He stood and gazed down at her. "Think of them as simple teaching tools for the course."

She placed the packet back in the box and stood. "I'll do that. If you don't need me for anything else, I'll see you later."

She turned to go, and Ethan reached out and lightly touched his hand on her forearm, stopping her.

"Amanda. About what I said to you yesterday..." He slipped his hands in his pockets.

"Which part?" She raised a brow. "You said a lot."

"The part about your life."

"I see." She lifted a small flashlight from the box and flipped it on, then off.

"I didn't mean to hurt your feelings."

She cocked her head to the side. "Who says you hurt my feelings?"

A half smile lifted the corner of his mouth, and a gleam of understanding lit his eyes. "You forget how well I know you, Mandy. I could tell I hurt you as soon as I said the words, *dull and predictable*."

She clicked on the flashlight and shined the beam right in his face. "Is that an apology?"

Ethan squinted and twisted his head away. He snaked out his arm and plucked the flashlight from her hand. She inhaled and took a hasty step back.

"For any pain I may have caused, yes, but for the truth of those words, no. Can you deny that your life is predictable?"

"Your words were more of an insult than anything else." She casually lifted her finger and pushed the glasses up the bridge of her nose. "I've thought about what you said, and yes, my life is predictable. My job certainly has a predictable aspect to it. There's no denying that.

"I have to be here at a certain time—the events of the day are scheduled to the minute—I get to leave at a certain time—then I have to come back and do it again the next day. Holidays are predictable, how many days I get off, and when I must return."

She placed her hands to her hips and stepped toward him. "But the events throughout the day can be quite unpredictable, and those random moments must fit in with the predictable structure of this job."

"My goodness." He laughed. "Take a breath."

"So yes," she continued as if he hadn't spoken. "My life has been one big predictable event, but dull? Not on your life. Working with these kids, getting to know them like I have, seeing them at church, going to their ballgames and dance recitals—I wouldn't trade any of it for whatever it is that you've been doing the past couple of years. I've been nurturing young people, instilling values in them that I hope will last a lifetime."

She jabbed a finger to his chest. "There was a time when your photojournalism opened the eyes of the ignorant to the plight of so many people," she carelessly plunged on without missing a beat, "to the joys and the marvel of this planet. What have you done since? Whose lives have you changed with *Knight Owl*?" she practically spat the words.

"This town, this school," she ranted on, "is my family and there's nothing boring about it. Now if you'll excuse me, I need to go back to the office and start my predictable day."

"So that's what it's like to be firmly and irrevocably put in one's place?" Ethan halted her with his words. The lively twinkle in his eye incensed her even more.

It was all she could do not to lash out again, but knowing he would enjoy any further outburst kept her in check.

"It's no wonder you were chosen to be a school principal. Your talent for *no holds barred, telling it like it is,* repartee must please the parents to no end."

Chapter 14

Several more of Ethan's supplies arrived on Friday after lunch. Amanda noticed the boxes in the foyer on her way to the break room. She hadn't seen him since her dramatic exit the day before, and frankly, had no interest in engaging him any more than she had to. Better to shoot him a text and disappear.

She'd just started to text Ethan when a set of men's shoes and navy slacks entered her peripheral vision. She paused and glanced left.

"Ethan, I was just texting you. More of your supplies arrived."

"I know."

"How could—"

He held up his phone. "Got a text from Amazon."

"Oh."

"Sorry you had to deal with it," he said.

"It's no problem. All in a day's predictable work." She bent down and picked up the lighter of the three boxes, then stood.

"*Touché*, Miss Marsh." Ethan grinned and stacked the two heaviest boxes in his arms, then followed her to the storage room.

They deposited them in the corner with the others. "Thanks for your help, Mandy."

"Please don't call me that."

"But I've always called you that."

"That was then, and—"

"I know, I know." He threw up his hands. "And this is now."

"Exactly." She glanced at the mounds of boxes, then back at him. The sooner she helped him, the sooner he'd leave. "Do you want help unloading them?"

"Sure."

Ethan flicked opened his knife and carefully slid the blade across the top. After he maneuvered the container toward Amanda, she peeled back the flaps and proceeded to unload the supplies. They went through this process until they'd organized everything on the low table.

She pulled out a package of whistles of several different colors. She plucked out a blue one, put it to her lips, and blew. The unexpected high-pitched shrill pierced the small room. Ethan jumped, swore, and rounded on her. "What the—"

"Sorry." Amanda tried to suppress a giggle, but it bubbled up in spite of her efforts. "I just wanted to see how they sounded." She lowered the whistle to her lap. "I'm thinking of ordering more of these for the P.E. Department."

"Next time, let a body know before you attempt to destroy his hearing."

"Come on, it wasn't that loud. I startled you, that's all." She tossed the offending article back in the bag, then lifted her hand to her throat.

"What's wrong?" he asked.

"My throat's bothering me a little."

"Gargle with a little warm salt water. That always works for me."

"Thank you, Dr. Knight." She couldn't help but smile.

"Ahh, there's that twinkle," he said. "I thought maybe you'd lost it."

She sobered in seconds. It would not do for him to see she'd mellowed a bit where he was concerned. Since his return, keeping a wall in place had been her only defense against her treacherous heart.

By the time Amanda had finished her stint at the school, her throat had gotten worse. She stopped by the local walk-in clinic on her way to LNO's office to have it checked out.

"Strep throat has been going around," Carol, the nurse practitioner, said. After a short examination, Carol swabbed Amanda's throat. Fifteen minutes later, Carol walked back into the exam room. "It's positive. I can give you an antibiotic injection or the tablets."

A hater of needles, Amanda chose the latter. On the way out, she stopped at the water fountain and took the first dose. Next, she called Annie to let her know she wouldn't be in that afternoon.

A headache began to throb between her temples as she pulled into her driveway. Once inside, she changed into her yellow-and-white-checked cotton pajamas. A quick rummage through her medicine cabinet produced ibuprofen and a package of expired throat lozenges. She took the tablets, popped one lozenge in her mouth, then climbed into bed.

Curling up on her side, she punched the pillow underneath her head and closed her eyes. As she sucked on the lozenge, trying to relax and doze off to sleep, she was haunted by a pair of magnetic blue eyes—eyes that held a questioning gaze—or a teasing light of humor—tormenting her at every turn. Each time he was near, her heart beat just a little faster as the sweet memories fought to push aside the painful ones.

* * *

Ethan glanced at his watch as he pulled out of the school parking lot. He had just enough time for a quick bite before his meeting with Preston Mayfield, co-owner of Leeds Capital.

Thirty minutes later, he'd polished off a fish sandwich at the restaurant in the Sea Breeze Hotel. Once the waitress cleared his table, he ordered coffee and waited for Preston. The recent Zoom call John Duncan had set up between Leeds Capital and Ethan made it easy to recognize Preston as he entered the restaurant.

Preston spotted Ethan's lifted hand and made his way to the booth.

Ethan stood, and they shook hands. "Nice to meet you in person," Ethan said. "Have you eaten?"

"I have, thanks."

"Is this booth okay, or would you rather sit at the bar?"

"This is fine," Preston said.

They took their seats, and the waitress arrived with a refill for Ethan and a second cup for his guest.

"Nice hotel." Preston doused his coffee with cream. "The gulf view from my room is gorgeous."

"We're very proud of it." Ethan tipped a bit of sugar into his coffee. "The beauty of the Emerald Coast, as we locals call it, holds its own against any other coastal waters around the world."

They exchanged a few more pleasantries, but Ethan could tell that Preston wanted to get down to business.

"We've done our due diligence on *Key News* and we're very interested," Preston said, getting to the meat of the conversation. He cupped his coffee between both hands and eyed Ethan as if trying to anticipate his initial response. "As I've already mentioned, we're actively looking to add to our chain."

Ethan fingered the coffee cup handle. "Why my paper?"

Preston sat back. "It's small, with outdated methods, which makes it a perfect candidate for updating."

"I've no doubt there's more room for growth," Ethan said. "The paper hasn't branched out for quite some time now."

Preston nodded. "Once a few critical changes take place, *Key News* will start making some money."

"Your goal at Leeds is to acquire more small papers?"

"Yes, small and medium size."

"The more papers you acquire, the more synergies you combine, and the more revenue you generate." A scenario Ethan could never create on his own.

"That's right. After reviewing the stats for your paper, we believe it would be an excellent fit for us."

"If I agree to sell, how will you handle the staff, and what they publish?"

"Typically, we keep as much of the staff as possible. That said, we do cut down to what is only necessary."

"We have twelve employees, so how many would you keep?"

The waitress arrived, topped off their coffee cups, then walked to the next booth. Ethan glanced up at her, nodding his thanks.

"We'd keep about five, maybe six. We've found no more than that are needed since we require syndicated articles to go into all of our papers throughout the chain."

"Sounds like the local news would take a back seat to the syndicated news."

"That's correct." Preston casually took a sip, then set the cup back in the saucer. "Of course, they can continue posting information important to the locals, like engagements, deaths, sports scores, that kind of thing."

"And *Key News* becomes no more than a copy-and-paste kind of job for the five or six employees left."

"I wouldn't quite state it like that, but..." Preston shrugged, "...that's one way of saying it, I guess."

Ethan twisted the cup between his fingers. "And its small-town charm will be history."

"Look, I can see this will be a difficult decision for you."

"I have to admit, I am concerned about my employees. Several of them have been with us for thirty years."

"That's not unusual for a paper in a town of this size. As much as I'd like to close this deal, it has to be right for both parties. Take three or four days to think it over—a week if you need it, then call me with your decision."

Ethan's meeting with Preston was sobering to say the least. He'd do what Preston suggested—think it over. He just hoped a week would be enough time, but somehow, he didn't think a few days or a week would make any difference to how he felt. Frankly, the details from their meeting made him more inclined *not* to sell. Which would lead to a whole host of new problems.

He was passing the school and decided to swing by to see if any more of his supplies had arrived. Amazon hadn't sent any notices, but he'd use any excuse to hound Amanda. He smiled as he approached Sally.

"If you're looking for Miss Marsh, she went home earlier with a sore throat."

"Oh. I'm sorry to hear that. Thank you for telling me." Ethan left the school and headed home. He pushed through the side door. "Grandma, do you have any of your homemade chicken noodle soup?" he yelled.

She entered the kitchen. "Yes, in the freezer, but I have pot roast for dinner."

"Amanda's at home, sick. Do you mind if I take the soup to her?"

"Of course not. Hope it's nothing serious."

"Sore throat." He grabbed a grocery sack from under the sink as she pulled the soup from behind the frozen peas.

"It thaws easily in the microwave," his grandmother said.

"Thanks, you're the best." He kissed her cheek and left.

Chapter 15

Amanda unfolded her aching body from the green-and-white floral sofa. Leaning forward, she lifted two large scrapbooks from the coffee table and placed them to her left.

She tucked her legs beneath her, unwrapped a throat lozenge and popped it in her mouth. She lifted the top scrapbook onto her lap and flipped open the hunter-green, leather cover to one of Ethan's first articles.

She didn't need to read them as she'd devoured each one many times over the years, especially those early days when she'd missed him so much. She'd lovingly clipped his photos and exposés from *GW* and other magazines, carefully preserving each.

She'd read and reread them many times, curious as to where he'd be off to next on the planet—only discovering his following location upon reading his next article and always wondering how things would have been different if they had gone to college together.

What an amazing gifted man. Each exposé, along with the

photographs, further evidence of his talent. Several of the articles had won prestigious awards in journalism.

She turned the page to the article on Mont Saint-Michel, a French medieval monastery surrounded by the sea. She shook her head. Ethan was as far from being a monk as any man. The 1300-year-old abbey was surrounded by mystery and so was Ethan for that matter. She wondered why he insisted on volunteering for the workshop at the school. There had to be some ulterior motive. Not for one second did she buy that, *interest in the community,* excuse.

She paused and unwrapped another honey-lemon lozenge and placed it in her mouth.

The next picture had always astonished her and not in a good way. The photo was taken when he'd received the *Sigma Delta Chi* Award for excellence in journalism. The tall, clingy, blonde at his side, who looked to have been *poured* into her little black dress, brought out the *big green monster* every time Amanda saw it. Even now, the sight of it made her insides churn. The small print underneath the photo displayed the woman's name, Adele Van Dorn.

She continued to peruse each page, stopping at one of her favorite articles. *Lions in Winter.*

A lion's natural habitat was in the warm tropical climates, and with the proper protection could live in the cold. The article exposed the cruelty of specific zoos and facilities in certain parts of the world that didn't provide the warmth and protection they needed during extreme cold weather.

Ethan outlined the mistreatment of those majestic creatures, revealing the lack of physical protection from the temperatures, snow, and other elements of winter. The most poignant piece for Amanda was the photo he'd captured of a lion and his lioness caged in a ten-foot square space blanketed in snow. Side by side, they posed, looking directly into the camera. The regal male stood with his glorious mane, and his mate sat nestled against him. It was both beautiful and heart-breaking.

She continued to pore over the albums, wondering how in the world he could give all of that up for that tabloid rag. It was only because of her research into his name that she'd even discovered, *Knight Owl*.

Something just didn't add up.

She placed her hand to her throat and swallowed against the pain. She'd sucked on more lozenges than anyone should have to do in one day. What she needed was a cup of hot tea with honey.

She'd just fixed her soothing drink when the doorbell rang. With tea in hand, she crossed the room to the front door and pulled it open.

* * *

"I heard you were sick," Ethan said. "How are you feeling?"

He wasn't sure if the sudden scowl on her face was due to his presence or to his foolish question. Or it could simply indicate how badly she felt. Either way, he was certain she was about to tell him.

"It hurts like the devil to swallow, I have a fever, body aches and pains, and a throbbing headache that refuses to go away." Her voice rose hysterically.

"And made all the worse now that I'm standing in your doorway."

"You said it," she peevishly grumbled.

"I'm sorry."

"I'm sorry, too. Look. This isn't a good time, so..." She

made a move to close the door, and he stepped one foot over the threshold.

"I know, and that's why I brought sustenance." He lifted the container of soup. "Ida's homemade chicken noodle."

She swallowed, and her face scrunched up in pain. "Is it that soup she makes with those small flat noodles and tiny bits of carrots and peas?"

"That's the one." He watched the play of emotions on her face. Mandy could never resist his grandmother's homemade chicken noodle soup.

"Okay, sure." She licked her lips. "I guess I *could* eat something."

"Good." He smiled. "If you'll let me in, I can get this heated up in no time."

Her shoulders sagged, and she stepped back. He entered and made his way to the kitchen.

"You just rest, and I'll take care of everything," he threw over his shoulder.

She put her hand to her throat and followed behind him. "I was about to have some hot tea, but I think it's gotten cold now."

He took the cup from her hand and placed it in the microwave for twenty seconds. After the bell dinged, he opened the narrow door.

"Here you go." He removed the cup and handed it to her. "Careful. Don't burn your tongue."

Their gaze met briefly as she took the cup from him. He'd gotten the impression she'd been about to say something, but instead, turned her attention to the container of soup.

The lackluster in her eyes told him how badly she must be feeling, and in that moment, all he wanted to do was hold her. Instead, he let his gaze linger on her hands as she set her cup aside to peel off the plastic lid of the soup container—the frown set between her eyes as she grabbed a bowl from the upper cabinet.

He placed his palm over hers. "I've got this." He took the bowl from her. "I do know my way around in your kitchen."

Ignoring him, she grabbed a large serving spoon from the utensil drawer and handed it to him. As he slid the frozen soup into the bowl, she ripped off a piece of paper towel and passed it over as well. "Cover the bowl with this. I don't want it exploding in there."

He captured her gaze with his. "I know what to do. Now go sit down and prop up your feet like a good girl, or I'll be forced to carry you in there, myself."

A stubborn gleam entered her eyes, and she glanced from him to the microwave as if weighing her decision. But when she glanced over her shoulder to the living room she gave a start, sucked in a quick breath, and stared. "You're right." She picked up her tea. "I do feel lousy. I'll take my tea and go."

Interesting. He knew instinctively her about-change had nothing to do with his threat to carry her. Curious, he watched her walk into the living area. Once there, she quickly picked something up off the coffee table and shoved it onto the floor underneath.

The microwave dinged, turning his attention back to the soup. He broke up the pieces with a fork, set the heat to another minute, then looked back at Amanda. She grabbed a decorative pillow and slid down along the sofa. *Good.* Maybe she'd rest while he finished heating up the soup.

The thaw process was taking way too long, so Ethan procured a pan from the lower cabinet and dumped the rest of the half-frozen mixture into it. He set the flame to low, grabbed a cold lemonade from the fridge, then joined her.

Before he got to the couch, he could see Amanda had fallen asleep. He stood still, looking down at her feverish, flushed cheeks. Even sick she was beautiful, with her tousled hair splayed across the pink pillow—her lips slightly parted—her breathing a bit labored.

Careful not to wake her, he sat on the edge of the sofa. He smoothed damp tendrils of curls off her brow, then leaned over and brushed a gentle kiss across her forehead. Certain she was asleep, he reached underneath the low table and pulled out two, green leather albums. He took the chair opposite the sofa, set the albums in his lap, and opened the top one.

Astonished, he merely stared. Of all the things he'd expected, it never occurred to him that she'd kept his articles. Not only had she kept them but also protected each one with archival sleeves.

He scanned page after page of his work, recollecting those amazing years with *Geographic World*. It had been the honor of a lifetime to work for them. He'd met so many talented people along the way and had grown up under their coaching and guidance.

He set that album aside and opened the second. The articles and photographs focused on his time as an embedded journalist and the atrocities of war, all of which had led to his decision to change direction.

He closed the leather cover and glanced at Amanda while he stacked the albums together on the floor.

Her breathing was still labored. She stirred as he contemplated waking her. A soft moan escaped her lips, and she opened her eyes.

* * *

Amanda awoke to the smell of chicken broth goodness. Her stomach followed suit with a deep gurgle of hunger. She yawned and gazed across the coffee table. Ethan was comfortably seated in the club chair opposite, watching her. She blinked and stared as the corner of his mouth quirked in a half smile.

"Feeling any better?"

She pushed herself upright and dropped her gaze from his. "You should have woken me up." She hated that he'd watched her sleep. Hated he'd witnessed and continued to observe her in a most vulnerable state. The satisfied expression on his face meant he knew it, too—knew it bothered her—and knew she'd rather it had been anyone but him to have checked on her while she was sick. But for the life of her, she had no idea why that fact should produce that humorous twinkle in his eye.

"The soup smells gorgeous." She forced herself to look at him. "Have you already eaten?"

"No, I waited for you. It's been simmering, and if you're ready, I'll ladle it up." He stood as he spoke and made his way to the kitchen. "Do you feel up to eating in here, or should I bring it to the couch?" he hollered.

"I'll come in there." Legs a bit wobbly, she stood still for a moment before crossing the room to the kitchen table. Ethan set the soup at each of their places, along with a plate of saltine crackers, butter, and water.

"What would you like to drink?"

"Water's fine for now," she said. Suddenly self-conscious, she glanced down at her lightweight robe over her shorty pajamas. She hugged the robe tightly to her chest, securing it at the waist, then took her seat.

"I've seen you in less." He spooned a mouthful of soup between his lips.

Her mind raced over the years and wondered what *less* he had seen her in. The only thing that came to mind would've been her bikini. She shrugged and spooned up the hot soup, savoring the aroma, as well as the flavor. The bits of onion, peas, and carrots, along with noodles and a savory broth, were completely satisfying.

"This just feels more intimate, somehow." She swallowed and pinched off the corner of a cracker.

"You in PJs and me cooking for you—taking care of you, *is* intimate."

Their eyes met. "The last thing I want."

He gave her a look of feigned *shock*. "Now is that any way to speak to the one person who brought you sustenance?"

"Why do you have to make all of this so darned awkward?"

He stared at her with the most deliberate and guileless expression.

"You know you are. Just admit it." She picked up another cracker and buttered it so forcefully it broke to pieces. She stared at the mess in her hands. Butter had gone all over her fingers, and she sat there staring at them. She wasn't normally such a klutz— *must be the fever.*

Before she knew what Ethan was about, he'd gotten up and was now down on his haunches in front of her. He took hold of her hands and began wiping them with his napkin, as if she were a child. And she, like an idiot, just sat there and let him.

When he was through, he stood and looked down at her. "All better now?"

She pressed her lips together and shook her head—*such an infuriating man.*

After dinner, he fixed them both mugs of hot tea, then followed her into the living room. He was right behind her when she came to an abrupt stop. She spun toward him, opened her mouth to speak, thought better of it, and clamped it shut.

The sheepish look on Ethan's face told her all she needed to know.

"You looked through them, didn't you?" she said.

He carefully placed the mugs on the table. "Do you have any coasters?"

She wanted to scream. "That table is so old—nothing can hurt it anymore."

"Yes, I looked through them. How could I not? Despite your earlier effort, it was obvious you were hiding something." He shrugged. "The rest, as they say, is history."

"I don't know why I'm surprised." She collapsed on one end of the sofa. "I never could keep anything from you."

"That may have been true when we were kids, but you're doing a good job of it now. For weeks, I've been trying to figure out why you're so angry with me."

For a moment, she rallied and met the challenge in his gaze. "I guess you'll have to keep on wondering." She picked up her mug.

"Between you and my stubborn grandmother, I'm sure I will."

Silence fell between them as they sipped their tea, cradling their mugs within their hands.

Amanda glanced at the albums, then back at him. "Do you have anything to say about those?"

"Like, what?"

"Well, if you have nothing to say, then I certainly don't." She shook her head and lifted the tea to her mouth.

"Yet something tells me you do."

"Are you telling me that all of those articles..." She motioned toward the albums. "...meant nothing to you at all?"

"Why would you think that? Of course, they did and still do. I'm proud of the work I did."

"Do you regret giving all that up?"

"There are days I miss it, but so far, I have no regrets."

She ran her finger around the rim of the cup. "Before I became school principal, I taught a summer workshop on your work with *Geographic World*."

"Seriously?" Ethan's brows lifted in surprise.

"Three years in a row." She hugged the mug to her stomach. "The students were quite impressed that you were a graduate of the school. Two years ago, one of the girls followed in your footsteps. She received a full ride to Florida State in journalism."

"That's nice," he said. "Thanks for sharing."

She raised a hand to her throat and grimaced.

"Is it time for your antibiotics?"

She nodded as he stood. "Where are they?" he asked.

"On the kitchen counter."

Ethan was back in seconds with a glass of water and her meds.

She held up her open palm. "Thanks."

"Go to bed and get some real rest while I clean up the kitchen." He stood over her, his beautiful suede-blue eyes probing in their intensity. "Once those antibiotics kick in, you'll feel much better in the morning."

Ethan, taking charge—he'd always been good at that. Taking charge of their activities during and after high school, taking charge of college plans and their future together. It had all been so exciting, and she'd willingly let him do it. Then, in a weak moment, she'd let his father take charge, too. She'd sent Ethan away, and sadly, he had stayed there.

CHAPTER 16

Ethan had just forked a strip of sizzling bacon when he sensed a presence in the room. He turned around to see Amanda standing in the kitchen, arms folded across her robed figure.

"What are you still doing here?" she bit out.

He lifted a brow. "You must be feeling better." He set a plate of scrambled eggs, toast, and bacon at her place. "I'm fixing breakfast. I've already eaten, so you go ahead. Coffee?" He held up the pot.

Amanda squeezed her eyes shut, and for one second, he thought she'd refuse, but she nodded and took her seat.

"I was actually feeling better until I discovered you were still here. I think I feel a relapse coming on." She picked up a bacon slice and bit down.

He took the seat across from her. "I hope you still like your bacon crispy." He nodded to her plate.

"It's fine. And I see you put cheese in my scrambled eggs... just the way I like them," she said with an exaggerated sigh. "I appreciate your thoughtfulness *so much*."

"I can see from the daggers shooting from your eyes that you don't really mean that."

"What is it with you? Why do you insist on hounding me?" She gaped at him with a wide, questioning gaze. "You must know I have no wish to spend any time with you."

"Yes. You made that perfectly clear at our first meeting at the school." He took a sip of coffee. "But I feel differently."

"She slapped her hand against the tabletop. "And I don't care."

"Yes, you do."

"No. I really don't." She shook her head, forked a mouthful of cheesy eggs, and shoved them between her lips.

"It's not as if Daryl has put in an appearance. Doesn't he care for your well-being?"

"I'll thank you to leave Daryl out of this."

"Look, I'm sorry my being here this morning has upset you. I just wanted to make sure you were better before I left."

She lifted a stubborn chin and glared at him. "If you think for one minute your ministrations on my behalf can make up for the times you didn't show, then think again."

For a second, he just stared at her. "Since you put it that way..." He gave a curt nod and stood. "Don't get up." With that he strode to the door and walked out.

Sheesh!

With Amanda, it seemed he was forever taking one step forward, and then two steps back.

* * *

Amanda swiveled in her seat and watched Ethan walk away...and just like that, he was gone. Stunned at her own thoughtless outburst, she kept her eyes focused on the door.

The glaring quiet in the house was its own reprimand. He was totally and completely annoying, but that was no excuse for her behavior. How could she have been so rude?

Tears filled her eyes and slid down her cheeks. She sniffed and swiped at them with her fingers. Her only excuse was that she still felt bad. With that thought, she stood and stepped to the counter, opened the bottle of antibiotics, and chased one down with water.

She glanced back at her half-eaten breakfast and realized her sudden loss of appetite was solely due to her hateful comments and Ethan's abrupt departure. Ashamed, she wondered if she should call and apologize. The thought of groveling left a bad taste in her mouth. She could just imagine the spark of humor that would fill his gorgeous eyes.

That image alone kept her from picking up her phone, but she was a decent person, known by her students and the faculty for her fair-mindedness toward others. So, yes, she'd apologize, but would wait until she felt better before doing so. She huffed a huge sigh, cleared the table, and set the dishes in the sink to wash later.

For the next two days, Amanda continued her medication and called the school office daily to check in. Sally assured her that Mr. Grady, the assistant principal, was back from vacation and for her to just focus on getting better. She received similar encouragement from Annie when she called. "Beth Franklin is manning the desk while you're sick."

"She's perfect," Amanda said. "And as your top model, who's also been through your workshops, she's a great asset for LNO."

On Saturday, Annie stopped by with a chicken casserole and her notes on the new session for LNO. "I want your thoughts, and then I want you to consider presenting this session to the girls. As school principal, it'll mean a lot coming from you."

"I'd be honored," Amanda said. "Frankly, I was hoping you'd ask. If my schedule allows, I'd like to do more than answer phones and set up supplies for the classes."

"Speaking of that, I talked with Beth about helping out at LNO, and she said yes. What would you think if I let her help two afternoons a week for the rest of the summer? You'd have more time for yourself that way. And since you won't let me pay you, she could use the income."

"I think that's a great idea."

Annie glowed with appreciation. "I'll let Beth know." She placed the casserole in the oven on 350 degrees, then left with the promise to check on her later.

By Sunday, Amanda felt like her old self again and decided to take a short walk on the beach. It was another beautiful day along the Florida panhandle. She spread out her towel facing sunward, then stretched her body along its length. Eyes closed, she soaked up the afternoon rays, reveling in its healing light. Twenty minutes later, she sat up and hugged her knees to her chest.

The emerald water glistened clear in the sunlight. She stood and stepped along the white, sandy carpet, enjoying the feel of the warm sand squishing between her toes.

Ethan hadn't returned since his abrupt exit three days earlier. Truthfully, she'd hoped he might. His workshop started in the morning, and she'd put off apologizing long enough. She'd have to meet him at the school to help him and Jenny with any last-minute issues that might arise. Hopefully, he'd get there before Jenny. Amanda needed to speak with him privately. Things were now more awkward between them. Normally, she wouldn't care, except she'd been the cause and that didn't sit well with her.

CHAPTER 17

Monday morning, Ethan arrived at the school for the start of his workshop. Amanda stood near the entrance, her hair up in that unflattering topknot. He wondered if she'd worn it that way just to annoy him. The fact that she was there by herself was encouraging. Maybe that Jenny person wasn't coming after all.

A petite young woman wearing white slacks and a canary-yellow shirt entered the building and approached them. She had shoulder-length blond hair and an engaging smile.

"Ethan, this is Jenny Peterson," Amanda introduced them. "She'll be assisting you with your course over the next two weeks. Jenny this is Ethan Knight."

After they shook hands, Ethan glanced at Amanda who wore a satisfied expression. He shot her a look that told her just what he thought of her little maneuver. The smile Amanda returned told him she was well aware of his feelings.

"We have your supplies ready in the senior-only room at the end of this hall," Amanda said. "Jenny will help you sort everything out to your satisfaction. Only six signed up—three boys and three girls. As you know, under normal circumstances, we wouldn't have been able to hold this workshop because of the low number, but since you've graciously supplied everything, the six will be sufficient to continue."

Jenny led the way to the senior room. Ethan entered last and was surprised not only at the size and layout of the room, but also at the relaxed furnishings. An assortment of club chairs, two sofas, end tables, and a coffee table offered a comfortable living room experience. A set of long glass doors opened to a small, simply landscaped courtyard with outdoor seating beyond.

"Nice," he said. "I wasn't expecting anything like this." He gazed across the room at Amanda and set his backpack on the floor. "So, this is the senior-only room. What's the significance?"

"Each year, the senior class provides a parting gift to the school," Jenny said. "Three years ago, the seniors raised money to create this space specifically for all future seniors to use during their senior year."

"Oh, right. I remember now." He glanced over at Amanda. "Do you recall what our senior gift was?"

"We bought five 40X to 2000X lab LED binocular microscopes for the science lab," she said.

"Wow, that's some memory."

"I was head of the committee who helped make the decision. Besides, I'm the school principal. I'm supposed to know these things."

"I see."

Amanda gave a curt nod. "Well, if you two can take it from here, I'll wait at the front door and direct the students as they arrive."

Jenny set about organizing the comfortable space while

Ethan went to a nearby classroom and selected a small, square table for him to sit on. As he carried it in, he noticed Jenny had all the supplies neatly organized at each student's place.

The first two students arrived within minutes after he and Jenny set up the room. Ethan welcomed them and told them to pick a spot. He waited until all six were present before introducing himself.

When the students entered, they spoke directly to *Miss Peterson* with a familiarity Ethan admired. She was certainly a hit with the kids, and he had to admit, Jenny had been a good choice on Amanda's part. He still wasn't happy with the situation. Once they finished the first session, he would figure out a way to make Amanda a part of the course.

Jenny instructed the students to fill in their name tags. Ethan hadn't thought of that and was grateful for the suggestion. It made it easy to address the students by name.

There was Mark, tall with blond hair and wearing an Apalacha baseball cap and jeans. Sitting next to Mark was Denise, a petite redhead with freckles. A short boy with glasses, named Kip was next. Stan, the third boy, had longish brown hair and a happy countenance, and he sat on the sofa across from the others. Lastly, the other two girls, Sandy and Laura, were both brunettes wearing jeans and sleeveless tops. They each took a spot and began looking through their supplies.

Ethan perched on top of the square desk to address the students. "It's great having you here this morning. I hope you're as excited for this workshop as I am in teaching it. This will be a basic beginner course and who knows, if it goes well, we might be able to extend it to something more advanced."

He gathered up his notes. "First of all, everything at your place is for you to keep. The backpack is also yours, and you'll want to store all of your supplies inside because you'll be taking it with you on the overnight trip. So, don't lose it."

At the sound of backpacks being unzipped, Ethan continued, "Okay, pull out your syllabus and let's take a look at what we're going to learn over the next two weeks."

The rustling of papers peppered across the room as the students turned to the first page.

"You'll find the methods you learn here can be applied to other areas of your life. The overall key for any proficiency in survival is to prepare ahead of time. That's rule number one. In the next two weeks, we'll talk about six basic skills, then we'll spend a night in Apalacha State Park applying what we've learned.

"The first basic survival skill is fire."

A blond-headed boy raised his hand.

Ethan glanced at the boy's nametag. "Mark, you have a question?"

"Are we going to learn to build a fire without matches?"

"Absolutely." Ethan's answer brought smiles from all the students in the room. "So. Why do you think fire is top of the list as an important skill?" He glanced at the faces staring up at him. "Just shout it out."

"Warmth."

He nodded. "What else?"

"Light," Denise said.

"To be able to cook your food."

"Good, any other reasons?"

"How about comfort?" Kip said.

"Yes. All of those are correct." Ethan slid off the table. "Now let's go over a few methods of making a fire."

It only took about ten minutes for the back-and-forth to mushroom into a fun, informative learning session. They took a break about halfway through the morning, then Ethan led them to the patio area and demonstrated a few of the methods of making a fire.

Once the class was over, the kids thanked him and Jenny. Every student had the next session's assignment in hand and their supplies neatly stored in the black-and-silver backpacks. They exited the room looking excited and ready to apply what they'd learned.

Ethan and Jenny followed the kids to the entrance and saw to it that they were either picked up by their parents or got safely to their own car.

"Jenny," Ethan said, "that was more fun than I'd expected, and I really appreciate your help today."

"I absolutely loved it," she said. "And thanks for doing this workshop. Except for my Girl Scout days, I'm pretty raw when it comes to all of this survival stuff." She held up her packet. "I'm anxious to read through this and to assist in any way I can."

Amanda approached him as Jenny left the school. "So. How did it go this morning?"

He glanced down at her, tempted to yank the matronly topknot off her head. Except for the odd run-in while in town, and when she was sick, he'd rarely seen her hair down since his return. But there was something else, something more than her hairstyle. It was her bearing—stiff and formal as if holding something back. She seemed unable to look him in the eye, which was highly unusual for her normal, forthright behavior.

Awkward, that's it. She felt awkward with him and he was sure it had to do with the last time they were together.

"Better than I'd expected," he said, still watching her intently. "They're a great group of kids, and I'm really looking forward to our next session. They quickly took to the subject, and once they got going, the back-and-forth was excellent. So, I guess I can't complain. My only disappointment is that you weren't there."

"Oh, come on. Jenny had to have been great." Arms folded —Amanda's gaze reached his eyes for only a second before dropping to someplace near his chin. "I'm sure of it."

"She's super and the kids love her, but I'd still prefer you."

She finally focused fully on him with her principal stare, then shook her head. "Give it up, Ethan. It's not going to happen. Now, if you'll excuse me, I have work to do before I'm needed at LNO." With that, she turned on her heel—

"Hold it a second," he said.

She stopped, slowly turned around, then looked almost through him rather than at him.

"We've been talking a good five minutes, and you can hardly bring yourself to look me in the eye."

She raised her chin and did just that.

"Except for now, of course." He stuffed his hands into his pockets. "Our last meeting ending rather awkward, wouldn't you say?"

Her gaze fell to somewhere around his chest. "I know..." She suddenly squared her shoulders and looked right at him. "I also know you're annoying as hell."

He grinned. "Guilty as charged."

"And even though I know you had some ulterior motive in coming over, I...I'm sorry. I shouldn't have said what I did."

"Now, was that so hard?"

She huffed. "Is that any way to accept an apology?" She spun around and walked back into the office, but not before he caught the hint of a smile. He chuckled, unable to contain his amusement. *We're back on track!*

* * *

Amanda met Annie for lunch at Pearl's Diner. They'd just taken the last booth on the left when Alice arrived with their water and menus.

"Hey, you two. I haven't seen you in ages." Alice focused her attention on Amanda. "And I thought you'd have more time to come see me with school being out."

"The summer hours do make for a shorter day," Amanda said. "But this lady hired me for the afternoons, so..." She shrugged.

"Annie, a slave driver? I don't believe it." Alice gave Annie a wink. "Except maybe when it comes to keeping our sheriff in line."

"Don't let him hear you say that." Annie chuckled.

"Don't let me hear you say what?" Levi had just entered Pearl's. He acknowledged Alice with a wave as she made her way back to the counter.

"Levi darling, what are you doing here?"

"Hey, Levi." Amanda gave a small salute.

"Hey, yourself. You keeping my girl out of trouble?"

"You of all people should know that's pretty much impossible." Amanda lightly laughed.

"Don't I know it?" Levi placed his left hand on the top of the booth, bent at the waist, and kissed Annie on the lips.

"Can you join us?" Annie asked.

"Wish I could, sweetheart, but I just came in to pick up my order." Levi stepped over to the counter.

"Here you go, Sheriff," Alice said. "One oyster po' boy, fries, and a large drink."

"Put this on Annie's tab," he said. "I'm in a rush." He saluted them and left.

Amanda couldn't help but smile at Annie's glowing face. She and Levi were so cute together and so much in love. A heavy weight settled in her chest. For the time being, she would have to live vicariously through her friends.

Alice approached their booth. "You ladies having your usual?"

Amanda and Annie exchanged glances and nodded.

"Okay, then. Two sweet iced teas, and two cheeseburgers with fries. And how you two stay so thin is beyond me," Alice mumbled as she grabbed the menus and walked off.

They grinned at the remark as Annie lifted a small stack of notes from her handbag. She handed one set to Amanda and kept the other. The top of the page read, *It's Not All About You*. "That's the working title if you still like it."

"I do. I think you should keep it just the way it is. The title alone says it all."

"You're right. It does," Annie said. "And there's enough nuance in it that we could go several directions. We need to think of more keywords than what I have here that we can use as we break down the message."

"I agree." Amanda lifted the page to read aloud what Annie had written so far. "*Respect*, *critical spirit*, and I really like, *own your actions*. I'd include, *say you're sorry*." She thought about how her need to apologize to Ethan had nagged her for two full days, but when it got right down to doing it, she'd hesitated. She may have backed out completely if he hadn't basically shamed her into doing it.

Amanda skimmed over the page as Annie made notes.

"What about *judgmental*?" Amanda said.

"Got it." Annie scribbled the word down. "Those are all good, Mandy. And I'm thinking *labeling* would be another good word."

The discussion for the new session went on for several more minutes until Alice approach the table, carrying their lunch. She set the tea, burgers, and fries in front of them. “Anything else, ladies?”

“I don’t think so,” Amanda said.

“I’m good,” Annie added.

“Well, make sure you save room for my key lime pie.”

Chapter 18

"The different ways to start a fire is fun, but this next survival skill is just as important," Ethan said. "Shelter."

Wednesday morning's class hadn't been nearly as exciting as the first. During the *layering for survival* part, sheer boredom crossed five out of the six faces staring back at him. That spurred him to get through it as quickly as possible.

"Excuse me, Kip," Jenny said. "Are we keeping you from something?" Kip, who'd been scrolling through his phone, smiled sheepishly and put it away.

Jenny smothered a grin, and glanced at Ethan.

"Don't go to sleep on me yet," he said. That statement perked them up a bit. "I call this segment the three Ps—planned, packed, and prepared.

"The first layer of shelter is your clothing. Pretty obvious, right, but you'd be surprised how many people go off in the heat of the day unprepared for possible changes in the weather. What you wear is important for the environment you'll be in or likely experience. Layering your clothing is key, whether you're going to a ball game or a hike in the Colorado Mountains.

"Now, my trusty assistant will demonstrate." Jenny stood in front of the little group dressed in shorts and a t-shirt. "As you can see, she's wearing lightweight clothing. Let's say she starts out on her hike, and as she climbs higher, the temperature gets cooler."

Jenny wiggled into a pair of jeans as he spoke, bringing smiles and giggles from the six. Next, she put a long-sleeved shirt over the t-shirt.

"Now she's reached the mountaintop," Ethan said.

"She must not be hiking in Florida," Mark said, drawing more laughter from the others.

"Exactly. But what I'm telling you is not just for sunny Florida." He nodded to Jenny who'd now shoved each arm into a sweater. "It's obvious a sweater isn't going to keep her warm enough on a mountaintop, so..."

Jenny immediately shrugged into a down jacket, a hat, and gloves.

"Now she's prepared. She's planned ahead, she's packed accordingly, and she's ready for the elements." He slapped his palms together. "Let's give Miss Peterson a hand."

The students clapped with more enthusiasm than warranted.

"Thanks, Jenny."

"My pleasure." Jenny stepped to the side, un-layered, and took a seat in the back.

"Taking the idea of shelter to the next level is building one," he went on. "For this next part, we're going to watch a short video presentation. I want you to take notes because when we're on the field trip we're going to build one of these."

He started the video, then flipped off the light switch. The man on the screen gave instructions on how to build a lean-to with debris found in the wild.

While Jenny walked the students out of the building, Ethan packed up the video equipment, a bit frustrated with the day's session. His head simply hadn't been in it. He lived and breathed the topic, but the sale of the newspaper worried him. He was definitely off his game.

During the few months he'd been working with the news team, he'd grown to like the people. For all of their quirks, they were salt of the earth, good-hearted folks who cared for their town, the paper, and each other. Having worked together for so many years, they'd formed a bond of familiarity and deep friendship.

In all the exotic jobs he'd held over the years, none of the people he'd worked with had become that close. Friends, yes, and some good friends, but once the job ended, they all went their separate ways, with only the occasional text or call later on.

How could he break up such an intimate group of people that had worked so long for his father? No wonder his grandmother fretted. They were her family, too.

"Everything okay?" He turned to see Amanda standing just inside the room.

"Yeah, everything's fine." He picked up the box of equipment and walked toward her.

She stepped aside so he could pass and followed him out to his car. "You don't seem fine."

He lowered the box in the truck and slammed it shut. "Don't tell me you're concerned?"

"You're teaching my students. So that makes me concerned."

He turned toward her and rested his hip along the back of the car. "My preoccupation has nothing to do with your students. Your wee lambs are fine."

"Then what is it? What's wrong?" She lifted her hand, shielding her eyes from the sun.

"How do you know something is wrong?"

"Back in the classroom...the faraway look in your eyes, the frown on your face." She dropped her gaze, lowered her arm, and ran her fingers along the hem of her blouse. "You haven't changed all that much. I can still read you pretty well."

He pushed off the car and held out his hand. "Walk with me."

* * *

Amanda hesitated as she looked between his open palm and the hopeful expression on his face. It had been years since he'd held her hands in his—hands that had squeezed silent messages between the two of them and had trembled with eagerness for his touch.

Would it still feel the same?

She slowly placed her fingers into his upward palm. His hand gently clasped hers. Immediately familiar, the warm grip tightened, but not too much.

He led her down the pathway toward the neighboring park. They walked side by side under a row of coconut palm trees. Neither of them spoke. She glanced at his profile, at his thoughtful face, certain he was measuring his words before they even left his lips. He would speak when ready.

They came to a bench and sat down.

"For a minute there," he finally said, "I didn't think you'd take my hand." His words weren't at all what she'd expected. He gave her fingers another slight squeeze, then released them.

She glanced down and gripped her hands together in her lap, hoping he hadn't noticed the heat rising in her cheeks.

"What else was I supposed to do with that lost-puppy look on your face? I simply had no choice." She offered a smile and waited for him to continue.

"Have I ever looked like a lost puppy?"

"Not to my knowledge, at least...not until today."

He blew out a breath. "As you know, I came home with the sole purpose of selling the family newspaper."

She stiffened at his words, and the reaction on his face told her he'd noticed.

"Of course, I made a slight adjustment in my reason for returning after the set-down you gave me that day in the parking lot."

The slow smile that lifted the corners of his mouth nearly devastated her resolve to stay neutral.

"But we'll save that discussion for another day." He became serious. "Anyway, I've been working with a man named John Duncan, he's a newspaper broker, and he's found two companies who are interested in talking with me. I met with one of them a few days ago."

"I see," she said.

He turned his gaze and stared at the row of bushes near the bench. "I'm not sure now if selling is the right thing to do. I was certain at first, but now I feel like a blasted yo-yo."

Her heart gave a jolt. "Did something happen to make you feel that way?"

"Not directly." He shrugged. "The man I talked with is Preston Mayfield. He's co-owner of Leeds Capital and very interested in the paper."

"Is it him or his offer that's bothering you?"

"He's fine. He seems honest and above board, and I actually like the man." Ethan plucked a leaf from the bush. "It's not him. We haven't talked money yet, so it's not that either.

Maybe it's the situation." He hunched a shoulder. "I'm not sure. As time goes by, I just feel like selling may be not be the best solution."

"What about the other buyer?"

"It's a company called Granger. The plan is to talk with them, too." He turned toward her. "Do you have any thoughts on the matter?" he asked with a somewhat embarrassed chuckle.

Be cool, Amanda. It wouldn't do for him to see your heart in your eyes.

She straightened her shoulders, put on her *head-of-the-school* persona, and cleared her throat. "Have you thought about talking to Ned? He's been running the business since your dad died. I'm sure he'd have some insights, and he may know something about Leeds Capital."

"I've thought about talking to him. Although, I'm not sure how involved he should be at this stage. I'd hate to build *his* hopes up as well as that of the rest of the crew."

"You've been here for what, seven, eight weeks or so?"

"A bit longer than that, why?"

"I assume you're getting to know the staff."

"Yes, of course."

"Maybe that's the problem. Maybe getting to know these people, seeing who they really are, seeing this *looming* sale from their point of view is what has made the difference...in you."

Their gazes locked and held.

"Maybe."

She glanced at her watch, breaking the hold he seemed to suddenly have on her.

"Sorry. I'm keeping you from something, aren't I?"

"I um, have a lunch date with Daryl, and then I head over to LNO."

"Right." They both stood. "How is Mr. Vanilla?"

She gave him her principal stare. "I'm not even going to justify that question with a response."

A glint of humor filled his gorgeous eyes. "You should stop by during the workshop on Friday," he said, as they walked left toward the school. "It's on signaling...your favorite survival skill." He grinned.

"I just might do that. I've always wanted to learn smoke signaling."

* * *

Ethan returned to the newsroom after his talk with Amanda and motioned for Ned to follow him to his office. He closed the door and sat behind his desk while Ned took the chair opposite.

"This'll only take a minute, Ned." He shifted in his seat. "I think I found a buyer." Ethan hated to be blunt, but sometimes, straight and to the point was the best method. Ned was a professional—he knew the score.

However, the look on Ned's face was not encouraging. His shoulders sagged and his face mirrored his disappointment.

"I'm sorry, Ned, but you knew this day would come."

"I know." He lifted his hands. "Just not this soon."

"I haven't said yes yet."

"Who made the offer?" Ned asked.

"A company called Leeds Capital?"

Ned nodded slowly. "I've heard of them."

"I met with one of the co-owners—Preston Mayfield. Here's his business card." Ethan handed it to Ned. "Between the Zoom call and a personal meeting with him, I think they might be a good fit for *Key News*. Of course, like I said, I haven't made a decision yet. I'm taking several days, possibly a week, to think about it. There's also a second company I may consider, but I wanted you in the loop."

"I appreciate that." Ned glanced at the business card.

"I could also use some help. The newspaper business is not my world."

Ned smiled.

"I see you agree." Ethan smiled back. "So. I wondered if you would do your own due diligence on Mayfield and Leeds Capital—see what you can find out."

"Be an investigative reporter, you mean."

"Yeah, something like that."

"Absolutely." Ned slipped the card into his shirt pocket and stood to leave.

"Don't say anything to the others about our conversation. I promise I'll give everyone notice before I make a final decision."

"I'd appreciate that, Ethan, and so will the others."

Ned left the office, closing the door behind him. Ethan sat back with a sigh. He'd made the right decision bringing Ned into the picture. Ethan hadn't been certain how he would receive the news, much less his request for Ned's help.

Ethan shouldn't have been surprised. The newsroom had been Ned's life for over thirty years. He was the classic newspaperman—a capable and talented investigative reporter. That had been his role at the Knight's family paper for almost thirty years, and the last ten as assistant editor. As acting editor, he'd done a great job with their small team of people, especially with the lack of resources available to them. Ned knew the score, and Ethan felt certain he'd thoroughly research Mayfield and Leeds. The last thing Ethan wanted to do was throw his small-town paper and its staff under the bus.

He pushed back his chair, stood, and walked to the front

side of his desk. He'd gotten one hurdle out of the way, but the closer he moved toward selling, the worse he felt.

Hitching his left hip along the edge of the desk, he watched the newsroom activity through the glass partition. Maybe there was a way the paper could stay in the family. With Ned at the helm, and bringing *Key News* into the future, it just might be possible.

Chapter 19

The following day, Amanda parked herself in a booth at the Green Parrot to pull together the notes for her session on LNO's workshop. She had almost two weeks before her presentation. Never one to put off work, she'd decided to take advantage of the slow morning at the school to knock out the first draft. She'd chosen the quiet atmosphere of the Green Parrot, believing she'd be less likely interrupted there.

She'd spent about ten minutes compiling her notes when someone called her name. She turned and looked in the direction it had come from and inwardly groaned.

"Amanda. Just the woman I wanted to see." Ethan walked to her booth like a man with a purpose. "Is your phone off?"

For a moment, Amanda could only stare at him. She blinked and glanced beyond him to see if he was alone.

"Yes, my phone is off. I only have one hour to work on this presentation, and I'd like to be alone and *undisturbed*." Her accent on the word only made him smile. He slid into the seat opposite her and rested his forearms on the table.

The waitress approached with coffee pot in hand. "Coffee sir?"

"No. He is not having coff—"

"Yes, please, with cream." He smiled at the waitress, then raised a brow at Amanda.

Amanda leveled him with a menacing stare. "Maybe you didn't hear what I said. I have work to do, and I'm not here to visit with you or anyone else, otherwise I would've grabbed a bite at Dairy Delight where there are throngs of people this time of day."

"I understand, and I promise not to take too long, but we have a problem."

Oh, no. "What is it?"

"It's going to rain this weekend." He tipped a bit of cream into his coffee and stirred.

"So." She raised her brow.

"That's when we take our overnight trip."

"Oh. Well, I guess we'll have to postpone it."

"Sorry, that's not an option." He took a sip of coffee and leaned forward. "I don't want to lose momentum with what they've learned."

"Then what do you suggest?"

"I'd like to double-up on the last session, and then leave two days earlier for the park," he said.

"What about the reservation?"

"I've already handled it with a park ranger. We can arrive Wednesday instead of Friday. We'll just need to get the parents' approval and hopefully, the kids don't have anything else scheduled for those two days."

"Fine...that's a good plan. If you're here for my permission, the answer is yes." She flicked her hand in the air. "Now, will you please go?" She deliberately focused on the work before her, hoping he would get the point and leave.

"What're you working on that takes that much concentration?"

"I'm leading one of Annie's workshops in a couple of—hey!" Before she'd realized it, he'd swiped the pages from her hands. She reached for them but only grabbed air. He relaxed into his seat and started reading.

"*It's not all about you,*" he snorted. "I beg to differ."

Amanda held out her hand. "Give those back, please."

He raised a brow. "That sounded more like a demand than a, *please*."

"Ethan!"

"*Respect others,*" he read.

She crossed her arms and shook her head.

"*Don't prejudge.*" He eyed her meaningfully. "How appropriate. Talk about perfect timing."

Amanda drummed her fingers on the edge of the table.

"*Watch that critical spirit*, oh and here's my favorite, *don't be quick to label others.*"

As he read through the topics with that slightly taunting attitude, she was reminded of the day she had sat in front of him with her most scathing, nose-in-the-air haughtiness, reading the topics of his workshop with similar belittling precision.

The amused gaze he raised to hers held something between reprimand and accusation. So, he, too, had been thinking of that day.

"You've had your fun, now hand them back and go."

He handed her the papers. "There's just one more little problem." The amusement in his eyes that mingled with a not-so-subtle gleam, should have warned her.

Now what? But whatever it was, he took his precious time in telling her. As if he savored the moment. She sighed, holding his gaze. "Well? What is it?"

"Jenny won't be able to accompany us on the trip."

Amanda tried her best to hold her irritation at bay. "Then we'll have to ask Margaret Simms."

"Jenny already asked her, and she is also unavailable."

Amanda's heartbeat stopped, then began to pound in her chest. She knew exactly what that meant but would make every effort to find another solution. "I guess that means we'll just have to postpone it until one of them can go on the trip."

"And I just explained why that's not going to happen."

She sat forward. "What about one of the parents?"

"And humiliate the poor kid whose mom has to go?"

"A father, then?"

"You're beginning to sound desperate." His eyes brimmed with laughter. "I can't believe the measures you're willing to go so you won't have to accompany me on this trip. Doesn't school policy for overnight field trips mandate two chaperones for every five students? Since there are six, I assume two more adults will be needed."

She gnawed her bottom lip and slouched back in her seat.

Grinning, he shook his head and pinned her with an amused stare. "You, Miss Marsh, will be accompanying us. I suggest you step into your *big-girl pants* and get with the program."

"Absolutely not."

He sat back, a slight curve on his lips. "Come on, it'll be fun. Where's your sense of adventure?"

She gave him stare for stare and sat up straight. "I'm afraid it left when you did."

"I see. So, we're back to that are we?" He folded his arms. "Woman... I left because you sent me away. That's the simple truth, and I see no reason to keep bringing it up. Our past has nothing to do with this dilemma. You are the school principal, and there's no one else but you who can go on this trip." A hint of a smile curved his mouth. "Don't forget, it was you who pointed out that pickings are slim in the qualified-female-teacher's department."

Of course, he was right, but that didn't make her steaming insides cool off one little bit. He was enjoying the predicament and that rankled more than anything, because they both knew she had no choice but to say yes.

"Why are you pushing so hard to finish this workshop?" she asked. "Seriously, what's one more week?"

He sobered, fisted his hands, and rested them on the table. "I'm now leaning toward selling."

"Oh."

"I need to finalize my...other commitments in preparation for what could end up being a quick sale."

She mustered a smile. "Congratulations."

"Thanks." He reached for the saltshaker and examined the lid.

She fingered the edge of the document on the table. "I guess you weren't kidding about that yo-yo affect. Seems all that concern you had yesterday was for naught."

"I'm still concerned. And my decision seems to spin with each new piece of information I get." He shrugged and replaced the salt next to the pepper. "Nothing's in stone. I'll know, when I know."

"Whatever the decision, I guess you'll be leaving again. Exploring the world, going back to exotic places, writing compelling articles...oh wait, you don't do that anymore."

He squinted. "Why is my work, or lack thereof, so important to you?"

"I've already answered that question."

"And yet you feel compelled to constantly bring it up." He picked up his cup and tossed down the rest of his coffee. The loud thud of the ceramic mug on the table made her jump. Jaw clenched, he held her gaze as he slid from the booth. The look he gave her held more irritation than anger—as if he could happily wring her neck.

"I have to let this play out—see where it goes," he said. "I have Ned looking into the company, as you suggested. Whatever he finds out will be added to the mix."

She dropped her gaze from his, adjusting the papers in front of her. "Right." She inhaled, then slowly released her breath. "I'll take Jenny's place. Just tell me what time and where I need to be, and I'll be there."

"I knew you'd be reasonable." A captivating tilt caught one corner of his well-shaped mouth, making her heart lurch with an all-too-familiar ache. "You always were, you know—completely practical and reasonable."

"Don't you mean dull and predictable?" Better to seek refuge in sarcasm. "You knew when you sat down that I wouldn't have any choice in the matter. And yet—"

"On the contrary. You had a choice, but when you saw it wasn't reasonable you—"

"Caved?"

"No," he said. "You simply made the right decision. Not for yourself, but for your students."

"Except, in this case, it wasn't for the students' benefit, but yours."

"Since you weren't aware of that at the time, your decision was for them." He stuffed his hands into his pockets. "You've always put others' needs before your own. Believe it or not, your unselfish behavior toward others is one of the things I loved about you."

His confession caught her completely off guard. She sat perfectly still, unable to say a word. Except that unselfish nature had led her to send him away. Pity he hadn't recognized that fact then, or now for that matter.

He started to leave, then stopped. "As for being predictable, the day you sent me away was the *least* predictable thing you've ever done. Trust me, I *did not* see that coming."

Her breath hitched and she winced inwardly. His words and the look of regret on his face as he said them, tore a deep hole in her heart as she watched him walk away.

* * *

Ethan slid behind the wheel of his BMW. What was it with her? Could the woman not have one conversation with him without bringing up the past? What was worse, when she did it, he did, too. He let out a low growl, put the car in gear, and turned onto Coleman Drive.

They'd been kids, for crying out loud. *Teenagers.* From his experience, the last thing teenagers should do was commit to a life-long relationship if they weren't ready. It was obvious neither he nor Amanda had been ready. Now, he had become a different person and so had she. Both of them had grown into wonderfully experienced, *complicated* adults. To his mind, that was a good thing.

His grandmother knew something about why Amanda had been acting the way she had, he was certain of it. He had half a mind to drive home that very minute and demand answers. He barked a laugh. *Like that would get anywhere with her.* Ida

Knight was one stubborn woman and would never divulge something that was not hers to share. That left Amanda. Something deeper had been going on with her since he'd returned, and he was determined to find out, no matter what it took to do so.

Ethan opened his signaling class by explaining about the rain and the need for a shortened week, then got down to business.

He demonstrated several of the methods, then had the students pull their flashlights and whistles from the backpacks. Jenny demonstrated SOS with the flashlight and had them practice. The kids then each took a turn practicing the three blows from their whistle.

The school security officer rushed into their room. "Who's in trouble?" he asked wide-eyed and panicked. Eight sets of eyes looked up at him in astonishment.

"Oh, sorry," Ethan said. "Everyone's fine. We're just practicing—"

"Next time, how about a warning?" He cast a sheepish grin and firmly shook his head "Carry on." The officer left the room.

Ethan turned back to the group and they all burst into laughter.

"Remember, next time we'll be combining the last two survival skills," Ethan reminded the students as they packed up their stuff. "Make sure your parents sign the new forms and have them in the office by or before our next and final session."

Ethan felt satisfied when he left the classroom. His talk on signaling turned out to be the best session yet. He'd never worked with teenagers before, and he loved how they approached that day's subject with eagerness and enthusiasm.

Thirty minutes later, he sat in the restaurant in the Sea Breeze Hotel, pushed aside the remains of his lunch, then turned on his laptop.

He opened the encrypted email from his military contact. The message confirmed Ethan's suspicion that the cipher had been hacked and was no longer trustworthy. His contact stated he could be in Apalacha Key by Friday and would like to hand-deliver the crucial information.

Too many people knew Ethan in town, and his meeting with a stranger would only lead to questions. His fingers paused over the keys as an idea formed in his mind. He typed...*Apalacha State Park, Saturday at 0100. There's a kiosk with a map of the area near White Oak Campground. It's miles into the forest. We can meet there.*

Chapter 20

Ethan, the supplies, the bus driver, and all six eager students filled the smaller, type-A school bus while Amanda, Mike Simms, and Lindsay Thomas followed in Mike's small Honda Civic.

Amanda felt the two-hour drive to Apalacha State Park seemed longer than when she'd made the drive with Ethan. Sitting in the cramped back seat of the small car was most likely the reason.

They stopped and registered at the park office, then continued on to the campground. Amanda was thankful when they arrived and relieved to finally unfold her stiff legs and body from the hatchback.

She'd been so uncomfortable; she hadn't noticed the campsite sign until she got out of the car. Buckhorn Hunt—the primitive site with the *one* porta-potty. The next two days were going to be an absolute nightmare.

By the time she'd regained feeling back into her legs, the students had already disembarked from the bus and were in the process of helping Ethan and the bus driver unload the canvas folding chairs, tents, two large Yeti ice chests, and other camping paraphernalia.

She helped Mike and Lindsay unload the Honda, then took note of the surroundings. Except for the pristine lake, it wasn't any better than the last time she saw it.

She turned on her heels, marched to the bus, stopped short of the activity, and waited for Ethan to notice her. He finally glanced her way, and she simply raised one finger and motioned for him to follow.

His forehead creased as he made his way to her side. "I can see you're all in a tizzy, so what is it?"

"The students did *choose* this campsite, right?"

Light dawned and a spark of humor filled his eyes. "Look. I know it wasn't the one—"

"Did? They? Choose? It?"

"Of course. I told you I'd let them decide."

"Except you were supposed to show them the photos, and I have them on my phone."

"I went to your office to get you, and you weren't there. So, I described the two options in detail."

She knew from his tone that he was lying and even more certain when he looked at her with what she could only describe as faux sympathy. He even had the nerve to add a heartfelt sigh for effect. "It seems the wee lambs preferred to rough it," he said.

Amanda wasn't about to let the conversation end there. "You fully explained the differences?"

"Yes, and they assured me they didn't need a picnic table."

"What about the electricity? No way would the girls have said no to that," she spat.

"Oh, the girls balked at first, but they finally gave way in the end."

"I bet they did."

He tilted his head and looked right at her. "You know, you would be a lot happier if you'd unclench that lovely jaw of yours and relax. Look around you. They're having a great time."

Amanda did as he suggested. The students had gathered their fishing rods and were laughing as they ambled toward the lake. She spun around. "Did you warn them to watch out for alligators?"

"Yes. That, and then some. I went over all the safety measures with them in class and again on the bus ride over. They're well prepared for these next two days, and if you had come to some of my workshops, you'd be aware of this." With those parting words, he grabbed one of the poles and joined the students.

The bus driver informed Amanda he'd be back for them Friday at four. She waved him on and helped Mike and Lindsay set up the folding table for the supplies. Afterward, Mike set the canvas seats in a circle around the firepit. Occasional whoops and hollers came from the lake as the three of them worked.

"Sounds like they're having a blast," Lindsay said.

"Sounds like they're catching dinner." Mike laughed. "And I for one am getting hungry."

"I thought we had to catch our own fish," Amanda teased. "Good thing I brought along some eats. They may not share."

"Hey, we're working," he said. "That counts." Mike slapped at a mosquito.

"Here you go, Mike." Lindsay tossed him the bug spray.

Amanda had to admit later that day, that the fragrance of freshly caught fish frying on an open fire smelled heavenly. Much to Mike's relief, the kids had caught enough for everyone. Kip and Stan had used some fire-starter-plug thingy to get the fire going and tossed dried leaves and twigs into the small flame until they could add larger pieces of wood. Once going, Ethan gave them a thumb's up.

The small group sat around the fire on the canvas folding seats. Earlier, Lindsay and Amanda had set out the ingredients for making s′mores, while Denise, Sandy, and Laura gathered long sticks to roast the marshmallows. The flames from the campfire were now perfect for the group to gather around without getting too hot.

A quiet flare of Amanda's marshmallow caught fire from the glowing coals. She pulled it back, blew it out, then carefully removed it from the stick, sliding it between two graham crackers. She bit into the warm gooeyness and semi-melted chocolate, savoring the simple but decadent dessert, as sticky marshmallow adhered to her fingers. Content for the moment, she gazed around the little group. Mike and Lindsay had their heads together and seemed oblivious to the rest of them. The three girls had scooted the chairs together, their whispering and giggling embellished by the waving of their hands and their animated faces.

A gentle breeze floated across the campsite, bringing with it the smell of the pines. She turned her attention to Ethan and watched him engage the three boys. They sat perfectly still, their young faces riveted on Ethan's as he shared a story from his travels. If only she could hear what he was saying, but he'd turned in his seat just enough so all she had was a side view and an occasional word.

The glow of the campfire played about his face, accenting his features like an artist's canvas. The teenager she'd loved had grown into one gorgeous, fascinating man. Dressed in hiking boots and jeans, he still held the small tree limb and tapped it along the edge of the fire as he talked. The snug t-shirt clung to his torso, highlighting his wonderful broad shoulders. Her gaze lingered on the arms that once held her and had drawn her close to his side.

Tears filled her eyes, and she hastily blinked them away. She loved him—and had never stopped. A sudden, desperate, raw ache pierced her heart at the thought of him leaving again.

"Okay, listen up you guys," Ethan said in a much louder tone.

His voice brought her back to the present.

"For the next two days, I want you to use, when appropriate, the five survival skills. Tell me again what they are."

The kids shouted out the five skills ending with *first aid*. "Hopefully, we won't need to use that last one," Ethan said. "While we're here, look to me for help if you get stuck. If you don't agree with each other about something, ask me."

He nodded toward Mike. "Mr. Simms has the tents positioned and ready for you to set up. We'll supervise, but you'll have to do the work."

Ethan held up a red sleeping mat. "There's one for each of us. But they have to be blown up by mouth. It takes a while, and it's totally up to you if you want to fool with it. I'll be sleeping on the ground, using only a sleeping bag. Any questions?"

"What's for breakfast?" Soft laughter floated around the campfire.

"Good question, Kip. Fish is the answer. Not only for breakfast, but also for lunch and dinner. I hope you have your booklet of edible berries and flowers in the wild, because you'll be forging for those tomorrow. We'll also be filtering our drinking water from the lake."

"We're drinking lake water?" Laura's face morphed into something close to horror.

"That's right."

"Eew," Denise said, wrinkling her nose. "Mr. Knight, are you sure that's safe?"

"I promise the water will be safe to drink. The equipment I've supplied here and in your backpacks is as good as military grade."

By the looks on each face, Amanda didn't think they'd sleep very well. "Listen guys, you can trust Mr. Knight," she said. "Don't forget, he's an expert at all this survival stuff. And he's drinking the same water we are."

Amanda glanced at Ethan, who stood watching her with an appreciative gleam in his eyes.

"Any more questions?" He looked out over the young faces and waited. "No one? Okay then, let's get to those tents."

Two fully assembled tents of different sizes stood at an angle facing the firepit and positioned far enough from the porta-potty for privacy. Mike and the three male students took one and Amanda, Lindsay and the three girls took the largest. Ethan had provided a single pup tent for himself.

* * *

Ethan rose early and had water heating over the campfire to make coffee. By the time it was hot, a line had formed at the porta-potty. Amanda crawled from her tent, wearing the same jeans and sleeveless blouse from the day before. The shirt was wrinkled, and he realized she must have slept in it. She shook out her long hair, then proceeded to put it up in a ponytail. She looked so cute like that, and he was glad she hadn't resorted to her schoolmarm bun.

She stopped abruptly when she spotted the line at the bathroom. The expression on her face mirrored something other than frustration over line-length. Ethan was still down on his haunches fixing his instant coffee, but stood when she hurried over to him.

"Please tell me you brought more than the two rolls of toilet paper I unpacked yesterday." Wide-eyed, she looked up at him. "Or are you planning for us to use leaves while we're here?"

"It would serve you right if I did." He poured hot water into a foam cup, added a teaspoon of instant coffee, then handed it to her. "After your glowing words of support last night, I thought you'd mellowed toward me."

"I didn't say those things for your benefit." She lifted the cup to her lips and sipped. "My goal was to ease their fears, so they could have at least one good night's sleep."

"There's still a line over there, so help me gather the fishing rods. If you want breakfast, Miss Marsh, you're going to have to catch it."

They stacked the rods against a nearby tree and Ethan checked the potty availability. "The line's gone, you'd better hurry."

Amanda did. A bit later, she slipped out from the tent as the group gathered the rods and bait. She'd changed her shirt for a blue-checked sleeveless blouse and had covered her head with an aqua baseball cap sporting the familiar Key Beach icon of a white sand dollar. She'd tucked her ponytail through the opening in the back, and when she walked, it swung delightfully back and forth.

She was adorable. His mind flashed back to when they were teenagers. She *still* looked like she did years ago...ponytail, ball cap, and jeans. Ethan savored the few moments he got to watch her as she took her place in line for a fishing rod. Seconds later, she looked up and caught him staring.

Good. Let her ponder that.

At least, he hoped she would.

He waited while the others grabbed their rods, then stepped alongside Amanda so he could walk with her to the lake. "You need any pointers with that?" He nodded to her rod and reel.

"I don't think so. Although it's been many years since I've gone fishing. I just hope I don't make a fool of myself."

"You'd better hope you catch a fish."

She cut a disbelieving glance in his direction.

"I'm not kidding," he said. "We each have to catch at least one this morning. I'd hate to see you go hungry."

"When did you become such a tyrant?"

"You ain't seen nothin′ yet." He gave her his best evil eye, then with thumb against finger, pretended to twist his villain's mustache.

"And you'd better not let those kids hear you talk like that, or they'll be calling their parents to come get them."

He laughed. "You worry way too much about these kids."

After the mornings catch, the girls had to start the fire for breakfast. The boys cried foul, saying they'd had it easier since Mr. Knight had already started one earlier.

"It was already out," Denise berated, wiping the powdery soot from her hands to her jeans. "We still had to go through all the same steps you did yesterday."

Lindsay went with Mark, Stan, and Kip to search for anything edible in the area. They came back with pine needles, a few cattails, mounds of clover, and blackberries.

"That's quite a stash," Ethan said. He lifted the pine needles and glanced around the group. "What do we do with these?"

"Boil them for tea," Sandy said.

"And the cattails?"

"Mark and I found a small clump near the lake." Stan opened up the booklet. "This says we can eat the cores of the young shoots or mash the rhizomes."

"But what does that mean?" Laura asked. "Do we eat them raw or cook them?"

"Let's try them raw." Mark stood and passed out the cores.

Laura took one bite, then spit it out. "Yuck. I think I'll pass."

"Trust me, you'd eat them if you were starving," Mark said. Laura made a face, further making her point.

"There's plenty of clover," Lindsay chimed in "Why don't we steam it over the fish?"

Mike smiled and seconded her suggestion, while Ethan exchanged a glance with Amanda. The sparkling humor in her eyes said plenty.

Ethan made his way to Amanda's side. "So. Mike and Lindsay, huh?"

"Sure looks like it," Amanda whispered. "In the past, I've always helped Mike with his journalism workshop, but this year he asked if Lindsay could help out—turned beet red when he suggested it, too."

"Looks like love still happens at Apalacha Key High School."

Amanda briefly raised her gaze to his, then lowered it to watch the students settle the grilling rack over the hot coals to prepare their meal. "The kids have really taken to all this. You've done a great job with them, Ethan." She licked her lips. "I'm sure that once the other students hear about the course, more will want to sign up, making it a regular summer workshop."

"I hope so." He cleared his throat. "I can't promise it will be led by me, though."

He felt, rather than saw, her scrutiny. Slowly, reluctantly, he met her gaze.

"That would be disappointing—for the students," she added quickly. "I can't speak for the rest of them, but I can clearly see you've won these six over."

"I like them, too."

"And trust me, they'll talk about this experience for a long time."

"I can always leave my class notes for the next guy." He turned his attention back to the group and walked toward them. "Mark, I want you and Denise to grab that bucket and get some lake water. Everyone else, get your water filters from your backpacks. I've already filtered water in the larger one, but I want each of you to have the experience of making your own."

Denise followed Mark as he carried the filled bucket back to the campsite.

Ethan waited for Mark and Denise to get settled, then instructed each of them on how to use their personal filter.

For lunch, they had more of the same...fish, clover, and blackberries. Afterward, Ethan and Mike took the kids into the forest to gather what they could use to make a shelter.

"Sandy, do you have a hat with you?" Ethan asked. "It's hot, and the sun won't be forgiving while we're working."

"No, sir, I forgot it."

"She can take mine." Amanda removed her aqua ball cap and handed it to Sandy.

"Thanks, Miss Marsh."

Ethan couldn't believe the stamina, enthusiasm, and creativity of the young people. It took all of that and then some to complete a fairly decent lean-to. "Good job everyone. Nothing like hard labor amongst friends." The kids laughed and moaned at the same time.

"You'll sleep well tonight, that's for sure," Mike added.

The kids were hungry after making the lean-to and couldn't wait to catch more fish. All went well until the fish refused to bite. At lunch, when the group stood around the fire with only three fish between them, Ethan decided to let them go for a good while longer with minimal food.

Amanda's glaring looks only got darker over the next two hours. He caught her eye and shook his head. They both knew there was plenty of food, and that he'd bring it out in due course.

Amanda walked over to him, took hold of his arm, and pulled him away from the rest of the group.

"These kids are hungry," she hissed. "How long are you going to wait?"

"You know my stance on the subject. They're here to learn how to survive. It's not going to hurt them to feel the physical pangs of hunger."

"I disagree."

"Disagree all you want, but this is my workshop. And let me assure you, skipping one meal doesn't suffice as *real* hunger. Not one person here has experienced true hunger. Trust me, I've seen it, and it's nothing like this."

"I know that." Her eyes flashed. "But we're not in some war zone. This is also supposed to be fun."

"I'm making a point with them, Amanda. Look around you. This forest is four hundred thousand acres. Any one of these kids could be lost out here one day. I want them to know how to make it until help comes."

She pivoted and marched away. He feared she intended to take over. "Listen up," she said. "I want each of you to go two by two and search for anything edible you can find. Take your booklets with you and really search, okay?"

She stomped over to the stack of rods. "I'm going back to the lake and see if any of the fish have changed their minds." She selected a rod and headed toward the water.

Ethan grabbed a rod and joined her, and she opened her mouth, surely to protest. "Two by two, remember?" he quickly said.

"Whatever." She rolled her eyes and marched onward.

He ignored her teenage response and stepped alongside her. "I told Mike and Lindsay to give them thirty minutes to search, then set the food out and start cooking the hamburgers. The smell should have them running back in no time."

She stopped midstride and looked up at him. "Why?"

"Maybe because you made the effort to allow my methods to work, even though you didn't agree with them." He tilted his head to one side. "Or, it may simply have been the anxious appeal I saw in those big brown eyes of yours. You may not believe this, but I have a history of succumbing to that particular look."

Her jaw dropped, making him smile. He gently placed his finger under her chin and lifted.

"What about these?" She held up her rod.

He checked his watch. "The bus will be here at four. There's plenty of time if you want to."

A sudden smile parted her lips. "Let's go fishing."

CHAPTER 21

The students weren't the only ones who'd come back to camp due to the mouth-watering aroma of beef sizzling over a flame. Ethan and Amanda, having caught zero fish, entered the campground as Kip stood squirting ketchup on the top half of his bun.

Ethan had to admit the feast of store-bought food being silently devoured by the young people was more than appetizing. Amanda had been right to insist on that addition to the overnight trip.

With everyone's appetite satisfied, the tents came down in record time and packed in their canvas hold-all's, along with the folding chairs. Leftover food had been appropriately stored with perishables in the ice chest.

The bus arrived, and Mark, bucket in hand, doused the remnants of the fire. He then spread the remaining coals with a limb, making sure the fire was fully out.

They all took their last turn at the rustic porta-potty before boarding the bus. Ethan had pre-planned to stay on his own a day or two longer.

Everyone boarded the bus, and Mike looked around. "Where's Amanda?" he asked.

"She's probably already on the bus," Lindsay said. "She told me she was going to ride along with the kids. Said the back seat of your car was a bit cramped for her."

Ethan looked up at the bus windows. He could just make out the sand-dollar emblem on Amanda's aqua baseball cap behind the second window on the far side. *Hmm.* Just when he thought things had been going better between them, she hadn't even bothered to tell him goodbye.

He shook hands with Mike and Lindsey, and they headed for their car, then Ethan waved goodbye to the bus as it pulled away from the campsite.

Ethan squatted down on his haunches and got back to filling his backpack.

"Where is everybody?"

Ethan froze—hands stilled over the top clip on the pack.

No!

He squeezed his eyes shut, then opened them while slowly turning his head. Amanda stood, wide-eyed, perplexed, and uncertain in the center of the camp, holding a roll of toilet paper.

"They're gone, Amanda. They've left."

"What do you mean, *left*? I'm right here."

"I can see that." Ethan stood.

"Where's the bus?" Amanda demanded.

I am not believing this. Ethan shook his head. "I just told you, Amanda. You missed the bus." He ran his hand over the back of his neck.

"What do you mean I missed the bus?"

"Repeating the question is not helping," he said.

"Call them back." Her voice rose an octave.

"We can't call them back. We don't have any way to do it."

"How could they leave me behind?" She began to pace, anger and frustration clearly evident in her every movement.

"We thought you were on the bus. You told Lindsay you were taking the bus."

"That's right." She stopped midstride. "I'd planned to take it back."

"We saw the hat and thought you were already on it."

She sucked in air. "My hat... I gave Sandy my hat while I waited for the bathroom this morning. It matched her blouse, so I told her she could wear it back."

"Between you informing Lindsay of your plans and the hat..." He had absolutely nothing else to say.

"And none of you thought to make sure that it was me on the bus?" she persisted.

"I guess not... But no reason to work yourself into a frenzy."

"I can't be here." A faint thread of hysteria filled her voice as she flung out her hands in simple despair. "I can't be here."

"Look around you, sweetheart. You *are* here, and there's nothing we can do about it."

Her dazed expression turned into one of panic. "Daryl is supposed to pick me up at seven. We're having dinner with his parents."

He looked across at her with growing impatience. "He'll have to take a rain check. I'm sure he'll understand." Ethan pushed the weight of his hand along the pack edge and zipped it closed. "Getting yourself all worked up will get us nowhere."

He stood and glanced around the campsite. "I have food enough for me. I'll leave half with you. If you want to chance staying here, in hopes someone comes back for you, then that's your decision. But I wouldn't count on that happening."

Her shoulders slumped, and she visibly crumbled.

"Unfortunately, you're going to have to come with me," Ethan said.

"Why can't we just stay here?"

"Because I have other plans, that's why," he barked. "I have a pickup scheduled, and it's not at this site."

"So, you do have someone coming to get you?"

"Of course, I do." He shrugged into his backpack.

Eyes wide, Amanda glanced from him, to the campsite, then back at him. He watched the uncertainty in her gaze—her flushed cheeks. She was in a quandary all right, and so was he. The last thing he needed was someone slowing him down. "Look, you'll just have to come with me. I'll share my food. It'll be all right."

"That won't be enough," she said. "I don't even have a fishing rod."

"I have one."

"Where?"

"I have a small one that collapses and fits right in my pack. There'll be streams and lakes—lots of opportunities to catch fish."

"How far away are we going?"

"It'll be dark soon, so about five miles—give or take." He secured the backpack strap around his waist and nodded.

"And the next day?" She visibly tensed, waiting for his answer, her gaze filled with something close to dread.

"Another fifteen or so."

"*Fifteen*?" she shrieked.

He glanced at her sneakers. "You'll be fine in those. It's not like we're going through rough terrain. It's pretty flat everywhere around here." He took in her jeans and sleeveless blouse. "I don't suppose you have a jacket."

"Yes, I have a jacket. It's packed on the bus. Where I'm

supposed to be." She ran her hands through her hair. "I was just letting everybody else use the bathroom first," she mumbled. "I just went to the bathroom."

"Didn't you hear the bus or the car start up?"

"No. I... I was in the forest."

"What? Why?" He stood completely still.

"I didn't want to wait in line, so I grabbed what was left of this roll of toilet paper, and I went into the woods."

"And you couldn't hear the bus from there, either?"

She licked her lips. "I went *way* into the woods. The thought of one of those students coming up on me while I was squatting over a bush..." She tightly squeezed her eyes and shivered. "I could never have lived that down."

He thought of her last campground bathroom experience and smothered a grin.

"Damn straight, I did. I went as far as was safe to do so." She held up the mostly used roll and shook it in the air. She suddenly stopped shaking it and stared at the roll as if horrified. "Please tell me you have more toilet paper."

He laughed in spite of his mounting frustration. "Yes, I have more toilet paper."

"At least that's something."

He glanced at his watch. "I want to make it to the next stop on my map, or we'll have to walk more miles tomorrow. I'm leaving now, but like I said, if you want to stay, I'll leave you half my food."

"You don't really expect me to stay here by myself, do you? And...and sleep out in the open?"

"Then come on. Let's go." Ethan did his best to ignore the scowl on her face. "We're burning daylight."

* * *

Amanda had no choice but to follow. She trailed after him, and a kernel of an idea began to sprout in her mind. Had Ethan somehow manipulated this disaster? Had it been his plan to get her trapped out there with him...at his mercy?

No. That was ridiculous. He, too, had been equally astonished at seeing she had been left behind.

She kept her gaze on his back and trudged behind him, keeping her focus between his broad shoulders and the path beneath her feet. Trailing behind him gave her a chance to observe. He was every inch a man, strong and self-assured. In a strange way, she'd found comfort concentrating on his dark wavy hair and how it still curled slightly at the nape of his neck. Much had changed with Ethan, but not his dark, gorgeous head of hair.

In an effort to keep up with his long strides, she started to take two steps to his one—an action that had her breaking a sweat. While panting for breath, the toe of her right sneaker caught an in-ground root, and she stumbled forward, careening into his backpack. Arms flailing, she grabbed onto his shoulders. He stumbled, then skidded to a halt.

He turned as she released him, his pack now hung askew on his back. "What happened? You okay?"

"Sorry. My foot caught on a root." She swallowed and panted for breath.

"Am I going too fast?"

"Maybe just a bit." She placed her hands to her knees and leaned forward.

"Let's take five minutes." He slipped off his pack and headed for the woods.

She glanced around, spotted a large fallen tree limb, and sat down. A few minutes later, he came out from the trees, and then shrugged into his backpack. "You ready?"

She wasn't sure if that look in his eyes was one of concern or annoyance. She was hot and suddenly thirsty, but she'd never admit either to him. Plus, they had only enough water for one. Until they reached a lake or a stream, she'd bide her time. She'd drink when he did and not before. As if he'd read her thoughts, he pulled a bottle of water from the side of his pack and handed it to her.

She stood, shaking her head. "No, thanks."

"I can go a long time before taking a drink. In my travels, I've gone a lot longer than this without water." He gazed at her with a gleam of understanding. "Go on, take it. You look like you need it, and if you collapse, I can't carry you *and* this pack."

She pressed her lips firmly together and all but yanked the bottle from his hand. He didn't move but waited while she took a drink.

"Keep it. Make sure you ration it, though. There're only four bottles between us, and according to the map, no water for at least four more miles."

With that, he headed along the trailhead that led them deeper into the woods. Amanda screwed the cap back in place and followed behind.

* * *

Ethan stopped in a small clearing and shrugged from beneath the straps. "We'll camp here for tonight." He lowered the pack to the ground and rested his gaze on Amanda. Her cheeks were still pink from the hike, the heat, and the humidity. Despite stopping several times to rest and have a snack, she'd barely had time to rally.

An hour prior, they'd stopped at the mouth of a narrow

lake where they filtered two of the empty water bottles and three narrow drinking containers made for hiking.

Ethan pulled out one of those and his set of stacked cookware from the backpack. He handed the pieces to Amanda. "Separate these and fill the small pot with about two inches of water. I'll work on building the fire."

She lowered her body to the ground. "Um...I could use some toothpaste. I assume you have some?"

He rummaged inside a small pouch on the side of his pack and tossed her the tube. "That's where I keep it. Just put it back when you're done and help yourself whenever you need it."

"Thanks." She put a dab on her finger, then inserted it with the paste inside her mouth. After several back-and-forth motions along her teeth, she took a swig of water, swished, then spit. "That is so much better."

"You can sterilize my toothbrush in the boiling water and use it if you want."

"Thanks, I'll think about it."

"There're a couple of low rocks on the other side of the pit. Not the best seating but..." He bent to gather kindling.

"This is fine for now."

He shrugged dismissively. "Suit yourself."

She ran her hand along the ground at her side and gathered a handful of Spanish moss and dried leaves. "Do we have to have a fire?" She tossed the bits of kindling into the pit. "It's so blasted hot."

"The fire will keep the four-legged, uninvited guests away." He gathered more pine needles and twigs as he talked, then added that to the fire ring. "And unless you want cold steak, I'd prepare that water."

"Steak?" Her eyes grew to the size of the small pot in her hand.

"I stored strips of steak and some other food items in the Yeti with my name on them." He snapped open a fire starter and had a nice blaze in seconds. "Do you seriously think I don't eat well while in the wilderness?"

Still seated on the ground, she gaped up at him. "Why you little fake. Are you telling me all of this survival talk is…is…a sham?"

"Of course not. I gave those kids real survival skills. Surviving means just that, surviving. That doesn't mean you don't bring the best food you can on your planned, outdoor adventure."

Once the fire settled down, he unfolded a circular cooking rack and centered it carefully in the firepit.

"So, are we boiling the meat?" She carefully set the pot in place.

"It's a way to plump the meat and heat it some before fully cooking it on the open flame. Then afterward, we'll use the leftover hot water to cook up some mouth-watering instant potatoes."

"Wow, all we need now is a salad." She leaned back on her hands and watched the pot.

"How about blackberries instead?"

"Man." She shook her head. "You *are* a Boy Scout."

"I try."

Ethan filled the single plate and handed it to Amanda. "You first," he said.

She took the plate. "I feel guilty taking this. You carried all the weight today—you should eat first."

"Nope, ladies first." He smiled.

A small, shy smile touched her lips. She lowered her gaze to the plate, forked a piece of meat, and placed it in her mouth."

"Is it cooked to your liking?" he asked.

She glanced up, the light of surprise in her eyes. "Yes. But you already knew that." She toyed with the dish in her lap.

"The past two days, you've made my coffee the way I like it, and now the steak. And when I had strep, you knew not only what I liked, but what I also needed."

"So, you've noticed."

"I've noticed a lot of things." She held his gaze, licked her lips, then focused back on the food. She scarfed the rest of her meal down, then handed him the plate. "I'm happy to wash it, first."

"No need. Conserving our drinking water is more important." He filled his own plate and made short order of the contents. "Now you can wash things up. Only be careful with the amount of water."

A twig snapped, followed by the rustling of leaves.

Amanda sucked in a sharp breath and spun her head toward the sound. "What was that?"

"Probably just a raccoon." He handed her the plate.

She took it and commenced the cleanup. After some hesitation, she sat down on the rock near him. *Well, it took her long enough.* He didn't think she'd ever come that close. He held up a cigar. "Mind if I smoke?"

She shook her head as a mocking gleam entered her eyes. "Let me guess... Cuban?"

"Seems you still remember a few things about me, too." He stretched out his legs and flicked the lighter over the brown, leafy tip and lit the cigar.

She leveled him with a confused stare. "True, but you didn't smoke anything while you lived at home."

"And yet, you knew I smoked Cubans."

"What else would world-renowned photojournalist, Ethan Knight, smoke?"

"You think you know me through speculation? And here I thought it was from all of those articles you kept." He turned his head slightly right and blew the smoke away from where she sat.

The low firelight seemed to enhance the pink flush that crept up her cheeks.

"For your information, I've always followed your career," she said. "As principal of Apalacha Key High School, it behooves me to keep up with our famous graduates."

Keeping his gaze on her, he lowered the Cuban from his mouth. "Is that the only reason?"

A wary look slowly grew in her eyes as if she struggled with how to answer.

"Stop looking at me as if I'm some specimen under a microscope." She frowned. "Please don't make this..." She waved her hands through the air. "...any more uncomfortable than it already is."

He drew on the end, tilted his chin back, then blew the smoke upward. "I'm not uncomfortable." Ethan held the cigar between thumb and forefinger and watched her. "As a matter of fact, I feel quite relaxed."

"Bully for you." She jumped to her feet and glanced around the campsite. "What are the sleeping arrangements?"

"Are you sure you're ready for bed? It's early yet."

"I'm sure."

He smothered a grin. "You act like I'm some stranger."

She shrugged. "I'm tired and would like to get some sleep. So..."

"What you're really asking is who gets the tent?"

There was that adorable pink face again, made more beautiful from the glow of the firelight. He sat forward and snuffed out the cigar on the ground. "You can take the tent. I'll sleep in the open."

"Thank you." The relief on her face was palpable.

"No problem. I've slept in worse conditions than this."

Chapter 22

Amanda had never been more thankful to finally crawl inside the pup tent. At least she had privacy. She and Ethan chose a flat area and removed as much of the ground debris as possible. He then set up the tent while she unrolled the sleeping bag.

"You don't have two of these by any chance, do you?" She knew the answer but couldn't help asking.

"Sorry, I wasn't expecting company." He stood from securing the tent corners and took the sleeping roll from her. "I'd let you have this, too, except it may rain tonight and this bag is mostly waterproof."

"What happens if there's a downpour?"

"Then you may find yourself curled by my side in the morning."

She felt certain his all-knowing grin was just for effect. Ethan knew the weather forecast for the weekend was rain, and therefore knew they would eventually be sharing the tiny tent.

"Thanks for the warning," she quipped.

The tent floor was clean but the ground underneath not at all forgiving. She tossed and turned, trying to get comfortable.

What she wouldn't give for one of those blow-up mats right now.

Her well-fitting jeans didn't help the situation either. She'd sleep better in the stifling heat if she could remove them but dared not with the threat of Ethan crawling in beside her.

After one more grueling hour, she caved.

"Screw it," she hissed in the dark, wiggling out of her jeans as quietly as she could. That definitely helped. As her body cooled down, she drifted off to sleep, thankful for Ethan's presence right outside.

Something pushed her, rousing her in the middle of the night. She moaned and rolled onto her right side. Another shove, and the feel of strong arms had her fully alert. She yelped.

"Move over, Mandy. I'm sorry but I need at least two feet of space."

"You scared me."

"The rain's moved in," Ethan said.

Suddenly aware of her bare legs, she tried to tuck them underneath her. Instead, the action caused her to fall into his arms.

"This is nice," he said.

She flattened her hands to his chest and pushed as hard as she could. "Let go of me and please stay on your side."

"That's what I was trying to do. I didn't mean to wake you up, but I had to move you over."

"And get that clingy wet mass away from me."

"I'm trying to turn it inside out where it's dry," he said. "I could use a little help, instead of complaints."

She unfurled one end of the sleeping roll, and they scooted forward together. After several awkward contortions, they faced the wet side toward the ground, leaving the dry part for them to lie on.

They took their respective sides, and Amanda scooted as

far right as she could while pulling the t-shirt down over her hips. It was no use—she'd have to put her jeans back on. She snatched them up, but the struggle to slip one pant leg over one foot proved impossible in the amount of space she sat in.

"What are you doing?" He huffed out a sigh. "Just lay down and go back to sleep."

Her mouth was dry, but the rain outside pounded the tent in rhythm to her racing heart. *Right.* Like she could actually sleep lying this close to him. She kicked the jeans back into the corner, sat up, then drew her legs tightly to her chest.

"What's the problem? I've seen you in less."

She rounded on him. "You certainly have not."

"You must have had more than a dozen bikinis. I never saw you in the same suit twice. At least here you're also covered in a t-shirt."

The fact that he was right didn't negate the awkwardness to his close proximity.

"Look Mandy, I'm tired, and I'm sure you are, too. So be a good girl and lay back down and cover up with the space blanket."

He placed his strong hands on her shoulders and pushed, and she had no choice but to lie back. He snapped up her jeans and began rolling and folding them into a make-shift pillow. She noted his set face, his clamped mouth, and fixed eyes as he slipped them underneath her head. Suddenly feeling like a child being tucked into bed, she watched him slip out the thin metallic-colored blanket from the plastic bag, and then, with a well-placed flick in the air, positioned it over her. "Isn't that more comfortable?" he asked. "You'll be asleep in no time. You won't even know I'm here."

The feel of his warm, masculine strength lying next to her said otherwise.

* * *

The rain had leveled off to a steady rhythm. Any other time, that mesmerizing pitter-patter would have had Ethan dozing off by now. Amanda had positioned herself as far away as she could. Hard to do with only five feet of tent to share, but she'd certainly made her point. The vibes from her rigid body had him staring at the tent ceiling.

"Would you relax?" he said.

Silence.

"Don't tell me you're worried about Daryl?"

"My only worry is that he'll be worried," she said. "I'm practically engaged to the man."

"The operative word being, *practically*." He rolled to his side, propped his head in his hand, and faced her. "I don't see a ring."

"I thought you wanted to sleep," she hissed.

"I do. I think we'll both have a better chance at that once we take care of this tension between us."

"What do you suggest?"

He placed his hands on her shoulders and turned her toward him. "Talk to me." She looked stiff and awkward. "Here." He slipped his arm underneath her head. "Isn't that more comfortable?"

"Yes."

"Good."

"Fine." She slowly released a breath. "You start."

"First." Ethan flicked on his small flashlight and hung it from the loop in the top of the tent. The soft light played over

Amanda's upturned face and gave him a clear view of her lovely, but taut, features.

"You know," he said, "since I've come back, you've treated me as if I've done something to you."

She turned her head and looked away from him. "Wow, you do know how to pick a subject."

"I get the impression from our conversations that it has something to do with the day I left for college."

"You left and I stayed. It's pretty straightforward."

"Yet somehow I don't think it's that simple." He tipped her chin with his finger, forcing her gaze back to his. She licked her lips, then returned her attention to the tent ceiling.

"After you left for Syracuse University, I thought we could make our long-distance relationship work. I never expected or wanted you to give up your opportunities." She lifted a delicate shoulder. "You were caught up in your world, and I was stuck here in mine. It didn't take long before your trips home became less and less frequent."

"I remember. But it wasn't until I got that summer internship with *Geographic World* that my visits really slowed. After I graduated and signed that five-year contract, my assignments took me to so many places with little-to-no communication. What was I supposed to do?"

"I know, but the fact remains...you didn't come back." A wistful expression covered her face, and the diffused light in the tent revealed the sadness in her eyes.

"I *did* come back—"

"Not enough to matter—at least, as far as you and I were concerned."

Of course, he could see how the prolonged distance had hurt her. "I was self-centered."

"No." She looked right at him. "You were focused on your

career. You had an amazing scholarship, and I didn't. I couldn't afford out-of-state tuition."

"I could've stayed and gone to Apalacha Key State College with you—gotten our degrees together. But you—"

She lifted her hand. "We both made choices based on our opportunities. You chose a career over a relationship, and that's not necessarily wrong. In your case, it was right. I don't regret encouraging you to go." She gently touched his arm. "That was a long time ago. We were kids, and there's no fault here by either one of us."

She gazed at him with a sincerity that touched him, but there was still something else. Something she'd left out of her pretty little talk, something in her eyes—pleading him to accept her answers and go on with his life.

He'd have to leave it for now. It was getting late. *We can continue this conversation tomorrow.*

"You're right," he said. "We were young. And I'm really sorry. I would never have deliberately hurt you."

"I know that." She rubbed her hands along her legs. "Look, it's late and I'm tired."

He nodded and removed his arm from underneath her head, then reached up and flicked off the flashlight.

Ethan woke early. The rising mist morphed into golden dust through the tops of the pines just visible through the narrow mesh window in the tent. Amanda's soft curves had snugged up against him sometime during the night. Ethan's chin rested on the top of her head. Being so close, he took a deep breath and inhaled the soft scents of lavender and lemon. He turned his head a fraction and kissed the side of her hair, then held her to him, waiting for her to stir. Until then, he'd simply enjoy holding her.

He thought over their late-night talk. Not much had been

revealed that he didn't already know, but she had definitely started to forgive him. Hopefully, he'd find a way to learn more of the story as the day progressed.

A soft and very pleasant sigh escaped Amanda's lips. She moved and opened her eyes. She arched her head to the side and glanced up at him.

"Sorry," she said. "I guess I got cold." She rolled to her side and pulled herself to an upright position. She ran her fingers through her long hair, then began to scoot forward.

"Don't go on my account," he teased.

That brought a smile to her sleepy, flushed, face. "Mother nature is calling." She grabbed her jeans and slid from the tent.

"Right." He followed Amanda outside. The sandy earth had absorbed the previous night's downpour, and except for raindrops dripping from the pine needles, there wasn't much evidence that it had rained at all. "You go right, and I'll go left, and then I'll meet you back here for coffee," he said.

Five minutes later, Amanda came out of the woods into the clearing, and Ethan had her cup of joe ready.

"Thanks." She accepted the pleasant gift. "Except for sleeping on the ground, I could get used to this." She carefully took a sip. "I had an eight o'clock class three semesters in a row. Before Dad died, he'd have a cup of coffee ready for me every morning. Without fail..."

"I'm sorry I wasn't there for you when he passed. By the time my grandmother's message got to me, he'd been gone for over a month."

"It's okay. I got your card and your kind note," Amanda said.

"I envied you."

She stared at him, perplexed.

"You two were so close." He ran his finger around the rim of his cup. "I would have given anything to have had that with my own father."

"It had been just the two of us for so many years," she said. "He lived a long, full life, and in the end, we got to say good-bye. Not everyone gets that."

He raised his cup, then downed the remaining contents. "I hate to rush you, but we have a long day ahead."

Twenty minutes later, they began the fifteen-mile hike deeper into the forest. That night, he had to meet his contact at 0100 hours. He hoped Amanda wouldn't be a problem.

CHAPTER 23

Amanda mulled over their late-night conversation as she followed Ethan onto narrow paths leading deeper and deeper into the park. Surprisingly, she hadn't been embarrassed at all waking up in his arms. She'd lain half-awake for several minutes before she'd decided to move. She had no desire to disturb him, but more than that, she reveled at his nearness and the strength of his arms as he held her—that, she had no wish to end.

She was curious, though. So far, he hadn't done anything but hike. As if the destination were more important than the actual outdoor experience. What was he up to? Maybe it was nothing more than a need to expend some energy and get back to nature, like he'd been used to doing before returning home.

The first stop of the morning was for water and another bathroom break in the woods. "Watch for snakes!" he called out as she went deeper into the forest. She welcomed the noise from a Red-headed Woodpecker drilling a hole halfway up the pine nearest her. His intense hammering made the forest seem less eerie.

She got back and found Ethan sitting on a small boulder, looking at his compass. He started to stand, but she lifted a hand. "I could use a few more minutes if that's okay."

"Yeah, sure." He pocketed his compass.

"Are we lost?"

"No. We're right on track." He glanced around. "Although, with the dense forest and narrow paths, it may seem that way to you."

Amanda sat on the ground, drew her knees to her chest, and fully focused on his face.

The corner of his mouth lifted, bringing a slight twinkle to the depths of his eyes. "What's up, Amanda? You can't be tired. We just started."

"Oh, I'm tired all right... Of traipsing behind you with little or no conversation—going deeper and deeper into the park without knowing where we're going."

"It's not my fault you got stranded with me. I told you—I have other plans—plans that don't include you."

"And those plans are?"

"None of your business."

"You're preoccupied. It's obvious you have to be someplace at a certain time." She pointed her hand toward the woods. "I just enjoyed the noisy company of a woodpecker. Did you even hear him?"

Except for an intense stare, she got nothing but silence. No, not silence—his eyes said plenty—nothing else would be forthcoming. And as if to make that fact perfectly clear, Ethan stood and, without a backward glance, continued on his journey.

* * *

Ethan attempted to slow his steps and ease Mandy's physical discomfort with a few more breaks during the day. In doing so, he would open himself up to more questions. He'd deal with those when the time came. He could handle her tenacious spirit—her persistent nature—and her aggravating interrogations.

Lunch consisted of a packet of tuna and crackers.

"We each get one?" she asked, taking the packet. "I thought we had to share everything."

"We're camping near a lake tonight. I'm confident we'll have fresh fish for dinner."

Ethan watched Amanda devour her lunch. He should have realized the long hikes would give her an appetite. During his six months embedded with the military, he'd grown used to going without and had survived those last weeks in the Ukraine on military rations.

If he'd known in advance that she was joining him on this journey, he'd have chosen a meeting place closer to the original campsite. The daylong hike was hard on Amanda, but somehow, she trooped on.

He forked a mouthful of tuna and eyed her. "No questions?"

She swallowed. "If I did, would you answer?"

"It depends."

"Why are you in such a rush? Are you afraid you'll miss your pickup?"

"My—*our* pickup has been instructed to wait."

"The Ethan I knew would stop and inspect his surroundings on a hike like this. Personally, I've never been this deep into the park. There're some interesting wildflowers here." She dipped a cracker into the tuna and popped it into her mouth.

"I've noticed, and someday, maybe you and I can come back here and tarry amongst the flora and fauna."

"Hum, we both know that's unlikely."

"How cynical," he teased.

She took a swig of water. A smile played about her full, kissable lips. It had been years since he'd placed his mouth to hers, and in that moment, he could think of nothing else.

"Tell me about the lavender fields," she said.

He blinked and stared. "What?"

"You know, the article in *Geographic World?* The photos alone conjured up their pungent fragrance and the descriptive words in your wonderful exposé only added to that fact."

"You always did love lavender." He smiled. "You used to make those little lavender posies."

She munched on a cracker and leveled him with a curious expression. "The article seemed out of character compared to your usual work."

"You may find this hard to believe, but I agreed to do the story because of you."

"Me?" She held a half-eaten cracker midair.

"As soon as I heard the words, *lavender fields*, I wanted to see them. And let me tell you, the photos do not do justice to the real vision. The fragrance is remarkable. I thought of you the whole time and wished you were there with me."

"An honest answer, for once." She shoved the rest of the cracker between her lips.

"I haven't lied to you." It was important she know that. There was enough mystery in the current circumstances without adding lies to the relationship. "I may not always tell you the whole story, but I've never lied to you."

She swallowed and sat, obviously speechless. The rebuke in his tone must have stung if the pink flush peppering her cheeks was any indication.

He checked his watch and stood. "Time to go." He shrugged into the backpack and waited for her to stand.

She scurried to her feet and brushed the pine needles and dirt from the seat of her pants. "Ethan, I didn't mean to insult you."

"I know." He cinched the front strap snugly at his waist and started walking.

They'd plowed through dense forest along narrow paths most of the day and had taken several more breaks, which put them in camp later than he'd planned.

Since the previous day, he'd parried her forthright questions as well as the subtle ones with the skill of a fencer's saber. He had questions, too. And that night, after dinner, he would ask them.

As to how he'd get away to meet his contact without her knowledge was another matter. The scheduled meeting was for 0100 hours at the White Oak campground. Hopefully, Amanda would be sound asleep by then.

They'd come upon the clearing about an hour before sunset. It was one of the most primitive campsites in the park, the firepit the only sign that anyone had ever camped there.

Amanda looked about ready to melt. Drops of moisture clung to her forehead and upper lip. The high humidity throughout the day had taken a toll on him as well. "I'm for a quick dip in the lake. It's safer if we go in together. Makes it easier to watch for snakes and alligators."

Amanda's flushed face registered surprise, but she didn't say no to his suggestion. She licked her lips. "Okay."

"Come on. If we're going in, we need to do it before dark." Amanda hesitated for a second, but followed behind him as he made his way toward the water. As he stripped down to his underwear, an Egret took flight from the other side of the lake. Ethan took a brief look at Amanda over his shoulder, then waded in.

Amanda walked to the edge and slipped off her jeans and shirt. Her eyes were round and observant as she stepped into the lake edge. A few more steps, and she lowered her torso, paddling to his side.

"That's far enough." He ran his hands through his hair. "We might need a quick exit."

Amanda dropped fully into the cool water, tilting her head back as she came to the surface. She stood fully upright and planted her feet on the sandy floor of the lake, not too far from where he was standing. She ran her hands over her wet head, pushing her hair away from her face. "You were right. This is heavenly. I hope we don't scare the fish away."

"No chance of that." He smiled. "I bet this lake hasn't seen a rod or reel for a long time. We should have a feast tonight."

She crossed her arms over her chest. "That would be lovely."

Amanda seemed to be having trouble looking directly at him. Surely, she wasn't getting all shy? Whatever it was, they were in the middle of a four hundred thousand acre state forest —in a lake—in their underwear. The situation was probably more of a big deal to her than it was to him.

Clear drops of water glistening on her eyelashes added a sweet, vulnerable appeal that made him long to protect her. The straps of her pink bra cut tightly into her flesh, and he wondered what she would do if he slipped one from her shoulder. She ran her hands up and down her arms and shivered.

"You're cold?"

"A bit."

"I'd be happy to warm you up."

Her eyes grew to enormous proportions.

"For crying out loud, you slept in my arms last night. Frankly, I don't see any difference."

"Last night was a mistake. This would be by choice."

He smiled and shook his head. "How about I choose for you." He closed the gap between them. "Your words say one thing, but your eyes, Miss Marsh, are telling a different story."

The dusty ceiling of sky peppered forth with the first visible stars of the evening as he slipped his hands up her arms, drawing her closer. The fact she didn't resist was a good sign. He encircled her waist with one arm and lifted his free hand. He trailed his finger down her wet cheek, then to her bra strap. She sucked in a quick breath when he pushed the strap aside. He gazed into her wide eyes.

She trembled, and he wondered if it was due to the cold water or because she was in his arms. He hoped the latter. He lowered his head and placed a delicate kiss on her shoulder. He then trailed his mouth upward to the base of her left ear, where he brushed his lips against the heart-shaped birthmark that had begged for a kiss since that day in Dairy Delight. He lifted his head, and as his gaze searched her face, he replaced the bra strap. The sweet, wistful longing in Amanda's eyes was all the invitation he needed.

He slowly descended his lips to meet hers, pliant and warm beneath his own—lingering—savoring—every moment. She raised trembling fingers to her lips when he lifted his head.

"What are you doing?" she asked.

"I think you know."

"Oh, Ethan," she whispered. "I'm practically engaged."

"So you keep reminding me."

She groaned, planted her hands against his chest, and gave a slight push. He released his hold, and for one second, their gazes locked, then he watched her lift off her feet and cut through the water.

After just a few strokes, she stood and waded the rest of the way onto the bank. He followed and strode from the water just as she snatched up her shirt. He pulled his t-shirt over his head as she slipped on hers. Both of them kept their jeans off as they walked back to the campsite.

"Why don't you gather what we need for the fire while I try to catch dinner." He pulled his fishing rod from his pack and unfolded it. "The fire starters are in the front pocket of my backpack."

He picked up his jeans, grabbed a flashlight, since it would likely be fully dark by the time he finished fishing, and walked back to the lake. After he slipped on his pants, he cast his line into the water, making sure he could still keep an eye on Amanda. She moved gracefully around the campsite, flitting from one spot to another, gathering twigs and dried leaves. Her wet hair had fallen loose, creating soft chestnut waves around her face.

Occasionally, she'd toss her head to keep her hair from her eyes. She was elegant and the picture of loveliness. She reminded him of a forest nymph—wearing only a blouse, legs still bare, her naturally wavy hair cascading around her shoulders, and the dense forest behind her.

A massive jerk hit the line, and he pulled back, his focus now on his catch. With the finesse of a seasoned fisherman, he'd met his match with this beauty. After a firm struggle, he hauled in the biggest catfish he'd seen in years. If he and Amanda weren't so hungry, he'd release it. He cast his line again, and in minutes, he caught another fish. This one was smaller, but between the two, they would eat their fill.

Amanda had a nice fire going when he got back. She was now dressed in her jeans and sneakers and sitting near the flames. She looked up when he approached. He raised his catch. "I cleaned them at the water's edge. The big fella fought hard, but he gave up in the end."

"He's huge, and I'm hungry," she said. "I checked your pack for something to go with the fish but couldn't find anything appropriate."

"Yeah, nothing left except beef jerky." He placed the fish across the pan, then sat back. "Our pickup will be here in the morning at seven. If you want, once we get back to town, we can go to Pearl's Diner for a hearty breakfast."

"Once we get back to town, I'm taking a long, hot shower."

Ethan chuckled. "I completely understand." He turned over the filet, added salt and pepper, then sat back. "Another three or four minutes, then we can eat while the second one's cooking."

"Sounds good. I'm practically drooling from the smell alone."

Between them, they shared the plate. After they'd eaten and cleaned the utensils in the lake, they sat by the fire in companionable silence, the crackle of burning pine and dying embers the only sound. He studied Amanda in the firelight. For the first time in two days, she seemed content. She held a slender stick in her right hand, drawing squiggly lines in the dirt with the tip. Maybe this was a good time to ask more questions. *Lord knows I have more than one.*

"What happened to you, Mandy?"

She glanced up, a slight crease between her eyes. "What do you mean?"

"What made you change your mind about us?"

Her hand holding the stick stilled, and she looked down, a soft smile parting her lips. "After last night, I figured more questions would be coming."

"Since the day I returned, you've implied that I offended you in some way. I've seen the hurt in your eyes more than once." He grabbed a handful of dried pine needs and tossed them into the flames. "*You* sent me away, and yet I've been made to feel like I'm the one who did something wrong."

She drew her knees to her chest. "My hurt has nothing to do with that day. It came...much later."

"You keep saying the words, *you didn't come back*. I feel like it's become your catchphrase."

She shrugged. "I guess that's how I remember it."

"Look. Even though I *did* come back—I realize now the short duration and infrequency of those visits didn't do a thing for our relationship." He fisted his hands together and rested his elbows on his knees. "You were right about that."

She tapped the point of the stick in the dirt. Even with her head turned slightly away, he could see the frown between her eyes.

"Look at me, honey."

Amanda turned, and her face held a pained expression.

"You thought I'd come back *to stay*, didn't you?"

"Yes."

"Why?"

She ran her fingers across her forehead. "At the time, I was a naïve, eighteen-year-old, who believed you would *pine away* for me and eventually realize you couldn't live without me." She lifted a delicate shoulder with a tremulous smile.

"I remember that adorable girl..." He smiled. "...and how she dreamed of adventure."

She turned fully toward him. "Ethan, *you* were my adventure." The light of the low fire danced over her serene features. "You know that, right?"

"Yet you sent me away. And since we're being honest... You crushed me."

"I know." Tears filled her eyes. "I could tell." She spoke in a low, barely audible voice, sniffed, and brushed away a tear. "But sometimes love is sacrificial."

The earnest appeal and her gaze hit a deep cord within his chest. She'd sent him away because she'd loved him. But how could she send him away like that when only days before they'd joyfully planned their future together?

If there was anyone who recoiled from making rash decisions, it was Amanda.

Something just didn't add up.

"I can still hear you saying, *it's a once in a lifetime opportunity*. It's as if you'd echoed my father with those words."

A sudden light of understanding hit him. Was it possible his father had something to do with her change of heart? *No.* She would never have listened to him.

"And didn't it turn out to be?" she asked.

Her question brought him back to the moment. "Yes, it did."

She crossed her legs, clasped her hands in her lap, and leaned closer. "You've made such an amazing name for yourself. You are truly gifted, Ethan, and if you would've come back here, who knows how your life and career would've turned out? We just wanted the best for you."

"You've changed, too. You've learned to hold that sassy tongue of yours."

A tiny giggle escaped her sweet mouth, accompanied by an adorable lowering of her eyelashes. Her cheeks glowed in the firelight, enhancing the pink flush certain to be there.

"And to temper your words. Even now, you share only so much before you stop." He pinned her with a meaningful stare.

A delicate lift of her shoulder was her only response.

"All kidding aside, you're still a beautiful woman—honest,

hardworking, faithful. I've seen the way you work with those teenagers. It's easy to see why they love and respect you."

Her gazed flickered somewhere over his shoulder. "I do love being a part of their lives. I guess I see a little bit of myself in them. Their excitement for the future, their crushes—so obvious, if they but knew it." She chuckled, a sweet laugh that tumbled from her lips like honey.

He got up and moved to her side. "Whether or not I should've come back is a moot point. I'm here now."

"Yes, but as soon as you sell the paper you're going to leave again."

"Amanda—"

"I've moved on, Ethan, and I'm practically engaged to another man." She lifted a shoulder and the sparkle in her eye dimmed to one of sorrow, as if she'd lost something she would never get back.

He ran his hand around the back of his neck. "What you see in him is beyond me. Daryl's not for you, Mandy."

"How would you know?" The sad, lost twinkle in her eye immediately turned to one of aggravation.

"Because you don't light up when he enters the room." He lifted his hand and tugged her hair.

Ethan decided their evening of confessions had been enough for one day. At first, he thought he would have more of a fight on his hands, but she'd opened up with an honest, forthright response he hadn't expected.

He'd learned a few things that had surprised him. *Clear up the past* had been his grandmother's advice...and he'd just made a couple of inroads. But Amanda was still holding back. There was something else—a place where she refused to go.

He'd hoped to find out why she was so angry with him. He grew pensive. The few times she'd displayed real anger was when they'd talked about *Knight Owl*. Words like, *tabloid* and *rag*, proof she'd found it distasteful. It was obvious she believed he'd given up real journalism for it. She'd made it clear how disappointed she'd been over that decision and had come close to shouting out the reason weeks before in her office.

Their excursion into the park would be over in the morning. Once they got back, he'd have to find a way to keep the newfound communication between them going. It seemed the answers to his questions only led to more questions. And what the devil did she mean when she said her hurt came later?

Chapter 24

Amanda opened her eyes to the light of the full moon—with the man in the moon watching her. "Hello," she whispered, smiling up at him. His glow splayed over the campsite and through the little tent window, adding a cozy feeling to the small space. She lifted her wristwatch to the light. *One a.m.* She'd been asleep almost three hours. She shifted and settled back down, her hands underneath her head.

She yawned and thought about Ethan's question earlier that evening. It had surprised her and was not at all the one she'd expected. *What happened to you?* She'd asked that same question over the years, pondering it more than once herself. And as to the part about adventure, she'd answered that as honestly as she could.

Amanda understood Ethan's love for travel and exploration. After she'd dealt with the fact that they were through as a couple, she'd settled into her life and had kept up with him through his articles.

In her own way, she'd continued her adventure with him

through his exploits across the world. Completely lame on her part, but there it was.

In the beginning, she'd thought he'd come back for her. She just knew he'd find a way. If he had, she'd have gladly gone with him, knowing she could finish her degree later. Together they'd work on his career and she'd be the *woman* behind the man.

She touched her fingers to her mouth, reliving his sweet kisses in the lake. *Dearest Ethan.* She sat up and scooted to the opening, unzipped the canvas, then lifted the flap.

He was gone.

The sleeping bag was still spread out on the ground and the campfire smoldered just beyond, but Ethan was nowhere in sight.

"Ethan?" she whispered into the dark.

She crawled from the tent and stood. "Ethan?" She waited a moment; certain he'd gone for a bathroom break. After several long minutes, she ducked inside the tent and slipped on her jeans and sneakers. She had no idea which way to start her search, or if she should even attempt to do so, but something didn't feel right. It seemed way too long for a mere bathroom run.

Amanda, thankful for the full moon overhead, crossed the campsite, then stepped along the path leading east. She'd gone about fifty feet when she spotted a speck of light in the distance.

She paused midstride. That had to be Ethan, since he had the flashlight. She crept forward, and the path widened a little. After a few more feet, she stopped and looked through an opening in the trees.

There was a dimly lit sign of a park area-map, like the ones they'd passed during their hike. Ethan stood with his back to her, looking at the map. Obviously, he had *not* made a bathroom run. She hovered, contemplating her next move, and another figure stepped out from behind the sign.

She sucked in a sharp breath. *What in the world...?*

Ethan shook hands with the man. Seconds later, muffled voices floated toward her. *So, this had been Ethan's plan all along*. He had set up a meeting with someone deep inside the park. *Why*? Amanda tried to make sense out of the low voices —catching the occasional word—but couldn't. The man pulled something from his pocket and handed it to Ethan.

They stood, deep in discussion for a few more minutes, and when the man finally left, Ethan turned, leveled the flashlight in her direction, and abruptly stopped.

She froze, then ducked within the brush. He could not find her there. She pivoted and hurried back along the path. In her haste, she stumbled, reached for a limb, and righted her body. Concerned he may have heard her, she glanced back, her heart in her throat. She squinted, peering into the darkness. The light had gone—disappeared—and so had Ethan. A tingling shiver crept up her arms.

She assumed he'd taken a different way back, and her heart thudded in her chest. She had to make it back to the campsite before he did. A firm hand clamped over her mouth as she turned to where she'd come from. It silenced the scream that rose in her throat. Terror engulfed her. Cold fear gripped her heart. She twisted to free herself, but the man's arm banded tighter around her waist with suffocating strength.

"It's me," Ethan whispered. "When I remove my hand, you cannot make a sound. Do you understand?" He spat the words.

She nodded and sagged against him. He released her, spun her around, and lifted a finger to his mouth.

Shivering, she pressed her arms to her stomach and watched

him. The thunderous expression on his face bode ill for someone, and in that moment, she knew it was for her. He stood perfectly still on high alert as if waiting for the all-clear. After an excruciating minute, he swung his angry gaze over her.

She licked her dry lips. "Ethan?"

His eyes blazed in the moonlight. Without saying a word, he grabbed her left arm and hauled her back to camp. He didn't stop when they arrived. He marched her to the tent, lifted the flap, and pushed her inside.

She tumbled forward and scurried as far back as the tent allowed. "Ethan Avery Knight." Her voice shook uncontrollably. "How dare you manhandle me?"

Jaw clenched, Ethan entered the tent and crouched down on his haunches. The luminescence of the full moon streamed through the mesh window, infusing the small space with its light. Her heart pounded as she stared wordlessly at him, becoming increasingly uneasy under his scrutiny. Suddenly weak, she shrank farther back until her body pressed deep into the canvas.

* * *

Ethan knew his anger had been based in raw fear for her safety. But that still didn't keep him from wanting to rip into her. "What the hell were you doing out there?" he harshly whispered. "I thought you had more sense than to go prowling around the woods in the middle of the night."

"I—I woke up, and you were gone." Her voice shook uncontrollably as she spat out the words. "I waited and—and when you didn't come back, I went looking for you."

In his anger, he hadn't noticed her trembling body. Knees to her chest, she cowered against the back of the tent like a frightened rabbit, her anxious brown eyes glistening with unshed tears.

He scrubbed a hand across his mouth as his anger subsided. "When I leveled the flashlight, I could see you in the trees. The thought that he may have also seen you..." He pressed his fingers to his forehead. "I honestly don't know what he would've done. And I wasn't about to take the time to find out." He rubbed his hand over the back of his neck. "I'm sorry I was rough on you, Mandy, but my methods were the only way I could prevent you from yelling out."

"What in the world are you up to, Ethan?" Her words were slightly above a whisper. "Who was that man?"

"I can't tell you."

She turned her head to the side and, with a hasty motion, brushed away an errant tear, then another. Silence lingered in the small canvas space. She kept her pale face turned away from him. Her naturally dried hair curled in soft waves along her cheek. "I thought it was him." Her voice shook as she spoke. "I thought it was the other man who grabbed me."

He inched toward her.

"Don't!" she lashed out, and kept her eyes averted.

God, he wanted to take her into his arms, but by the way she looked, he knew she'd have none of it. "Do you know what I wish?" he said.

She answered with an angry swipe at her tears.

"I wish I had some cherry cream cheese ice cream to give you."

A deep sob broke from her lips. She threw her hands over her face and sobbed again. That's all it took. In seconds, Ethan maneuvered across the tent floor and gathered her into his arms. Amanda fought him, but he simply tightened his grip, cradling her head to his chest.

"One second, you were there and—and then you were gone." She sobbed against him, clutching the fabric of his shirt between her fingers. "I thought he'd hit you—knocked you out—" Her muffled sobs turned into soft weeping against his shoulder.

Ethan held her to him, stroking her back. "Shhh...it's okay. You're safe, now." He spoke softly and brushed her hair off her forehead. "I don't want you to worry, okay? In due time, I'll explain all of this, but right now, I need you to trust me and to stop asking questions."

Amanda's slender body shuddered against his chest as her tears slowly subsided. She sniffled and pushed out of his embrace. Reluctantly, he released her. Holding her had been sheer heaven. To give her space, he moved back and positioned himself in the middle of the tent and watched her.

It seemed an eternity until she lifted red-rimmed eyes to his face, lashes still wet from her tears. "I saw the man in the light of the map board. I couldn't make out much except for the patch on his jacket. Right here." She tapped her shoulder. "It looked military."

She was hopeless. "Did you hear what I just said? Give it up, Amanda."

"What are you involved in? Please tell me it's not drugs," she pleaded.

"It's not." He shook his head. "And it's nothing illegal."

She fingered the edge of her blouse and dropped her eyes before his steady gaze. "Do you realize the only things I know about you from the time you were away are solely from what you've written?" She lifted her eyes to meet his. "Could you at least fill in some of the blanks? Would you tell me about the time you were in Ukraine embedded with the military?"

"Like what?"

"Something—*anything*, I don't know." She spoke with a soft wail in her voice. Her question was an obvious attempt to keep him engaged.

He'd frightened her and he needed to address that. "Mandy, you know I'd never do anything to hurt you, right?"

She ran her tongue over her lips and nodded.

Ethan maneuvered his body until he sat cross-legged, hands fisted together. "Covering war was difficult and disturbing in so many ways. I saw men lose it over what they'd seen and journalists develop PTSD and other things. The phrase, *the horrors of war,* means exactly that. The atrocities, the tragedies...were hard for me to deal with long-term. I rarely talk about the details of what I've witnessed, but it was the longest six months of my life.

"I came back to Florida ready to sell the family paper and to shake the war dust off my feet. War, and everything that goes with it, had left me cynical. I'd left *Geographic World* to cover the war, but quickly learned I preferred photographing exotic animals and faraway places. While I waited for the new contract from *GW*, I did freelance work with the *Orlando Times*—not near as exciting, but neither was it dangerous. I'm afraid my cynicism came through in several articles I wrote, including the one on Sheriff Hawke. The only danger, it seems, had been in offending you."

Silence, poignant and tender, filled the tent. He kept his gaze clinging to hers, analyzing her reaction. Her teary, tawny gaze slowly morphed from fear and uncertainty to one of warmth and concern.

Amanda edged forward to her hands and knees and gently, almost reverently, placed her lips to his. Her kiss was warm and sweet, telling him how sorry she was for the darkness he'd experienced.

He saw the heart-rending tenderness in her eyes when she pulled back. Moments before, it had mirrored fear and despair. Love and longing, mingled with fatigue now glistened from their amber depths. This moment—with her—was about his undoing. It was all he could do to keep his hands to his sides. Having just held her made it all the more difficult. But her kiss was not an invitation to take her in his arms, rather a sweet and loving, *I'm sorry*.

She sat back and settled against the canvas wall of the tent. Smothering a yawn, she stretched out her legs, keeping them to the right side. "Tell me something else that I don't know."

"I'm now leaning toward *not* selling the paper." He shrugged. "I'm calling it the yo-yo effect."

She blinked back her sleepiness. "Since we talked about it last week, I've been wondering how things were going." She fingered the charm around her neck. "Does that mean you're going to stay?"

He rubbed his fingers through his hair. "I haven't gotten that far yet."

Amanda stifled another yawn, and her body sagged with fatigue. "Sorry." She tried to smile, but it fell flat.

"Don't apologize. We're both tired. Let's call it a night." He shifted his body to the front panel, then glanced back at her. "Do you want me to bed down here with you?"

She hesitated, and for a moment he thought she'd say yes —*hoped* she'd say yes, but she shook her head. "I'll be fine."

"Okay. I'll be right outside the tent. And I promise—no more late-night rendezvous. We go home tomorrow." He held up the flap and inched through the opening to the outside, then turned back. "G'night, Mandy."

"Good night."

Ethan opened his eyes. The sun already peeked over the tops of the pines. He glanced at his watch. Their pickup would be there in thirty minutes. He stood, stretched, and stepped over to the tent.

He lifted the flap. Amanda lay on her side curled up with the silver blanket clutched to her chest. Her face was still puffy from her late-night tears, and he hated to wake her.

"Mandy," Ethan whispered. She stirred and opened her eyes. "Time to get up."

She pushed herself to a sitting position and lowered the blanket. "I'll be right out."

A few minutes later, she crawled from the tent. Ethan stood waiting and offered her his hand. "You have about twenty minutes before our ride gets here," he said. "I'll take down the tent while you freshen up." He handed her the roll of toilet paper.

He had just finished storing everything in his backpack when Amanda stepped out from the forest. He hitched the pack through his arms, hoisting it onto his shoulders, just as Levi Hawke appeared at the trail mouth.

"Sheriff!" Amanda hurried over to him. "I'm so glad to see you. How did you know where to find us?"

Levi and Ethan exchanged glances. "Good to see you, too, Amanda. Are you all right?"

She nodded.

"Ethan scheduled this pickup with me last week. I didn't know you'd be here, though."

Amanda looked back at Ethan, her searching gaze held a hint of doubt mingled with confusion. He answered her unspoken question with a slight smile.

"You two ready to get out of here?" Levi asked.

Ethan nodded, and Levi waited for them to follow.

"Do we have to walk all those miles back to the original campsite?" Amanda asked.

"No," Levi said, "there's another pick-up area less than a mile from here. That's where I parked."

To say Amanda had been confused by the morning's events was an understatement. Throughout the mile walk, Ethan ignored her questioning glances, but figured she'd find a way to verbally ask him at some point in the near future.

Chapter 25

Amanda couldn't think of anything more wonderful than being back in her cozy, air-conditioned bungalow. The first thing she did was brush her teeth. Then she stripped down, stepped into a hot shower, and soaped up. Legs shaved, hair washed and dried, and smelling of fresh lemons, she slipped on a floral cotton dress.

Ten minutes later, she set the frying pan in the sink to soak and sat down to crispy bacon, eggs-over-easy, and pancakes. She cut into the warm, buttery confection swirled with maple syrup and took a bite. *Heavenly*.

She took her time eating. As she savored each bite, she spent a moment to respond to several phone messages. Both Mike and Lindsay had felt terrible about leaving her, but knew she was in good hands with Ethan.

She sipped coffee and thought about her surprise at seeing the sheriff. Was he in the know or simply Ethan's pickup? Maybe Annie had some answers. Her thoughts shifted to the previous night's incident, which culminated with sobbing her fears out against his chest. Ethan had asked her to trust him. There was still so much she didn't know about his years away.

Was he seriously leaning toward not selling the paper? He'd definitely struggled with that decision over the past few weeks. She had to remind herself that he was only thinking about it and nothing had been decided.

Did she want Ethan to stay? Was there still a chance for them? And what about Daryl? Their relationship had recently sagged. Her opinion of him had changed when he hadn't bothered to check on her when she had strep. He'd been more worried about getting sick himself than making sure she was taken care of.

In sickness and in health. If he couldn't demonstrate that kind of lasting commitment before marriage, then he certainly wouldn't after.

What was the use? She lowered her fork. She didn't love Daryl. All the excuses as to why it wasn't a good time to look at rings had come from her lips, not his. And how many times had she feared he'd present her with a ring...in a public setting. What would she have done then? She felt sick at the thought of humiliating him publicly when she told him *no*.

Daryl might be vanilla on most things, but when it came to his ego, he was loud and flamboyant. He was the exact type to bend the knee and ask for her hand in marriage in a public place. She needed to end things with him. Keeping his hopes alive wasn't fair. Especially now that her true love had returned to Apalacha Key, reigniting a love she thought she'd lost. She wasn't sure what she'd do when Ethan left again. She didn't think her heart could take it.

The doorbell rang as she started clearing the table. She crossed to the door and looked through the peephole. *Daryl. Talk about timing...*

Not ready to face him, she briefly hesitated to gather her thoughts, and then opened the door.

"Hey, sweetie." He placed a light kiss on her lips, then stepped over the threshold. "You ready?"

Amanda stared at him and searched her mind for what she'd obviously forgotten.

"Sunday brunch at—"

"The Sea Breeze Hotel—yes, of course I remember," she lied. After the past several days, her date with Daryl had completely left her mind. She had no clue how she would do justice to the hotel's amazing brunch, but she hadn't the heart to disappoint him. "Just let me grab my purse."

Twenty minutes later, they were seated and being served fresh-squeezed orange juice.

"I guess you heard about me being stranded in the State Park?"

"Yes, my parents were disappointed when you didn't show up for dinner. I called Annie that night, and she told me you'd been left behind with Ethan."

"That's right." Amanda sipped her juice. "I hope you weren't too worried about me."

"Not at all. You're a capable woman." He smiled. "I knew you'd be fine."

She stared at him, feeling slightly stunned at his dismissive attitude. Yet he continued on, oblivious to her feelings. She knew he'd meant his remarks as a compliment, but they only confirmed everything she'd been feeling lately about their relationship.

Daryl reached across the table and took Amanda's hand in his. "Now that I have your undivided attention, I thought we'd go to Walton's Jewelers this afternoon." He gave her fingers a slight squeeze. "What do you say?"

"Let's go get some ice cream instead."

Mouth gaping, he simply stared at her. "But there's dessert here. It's part of our brunch."

"But I want you to try my favorite flavor, cherry cream cheese."

He gave her an indulgent smile. "I've tried other flavors in the past, and I'm perfectly happy with vanilla."

"I know." She blew out a sigh.

"What's wrong? You've barely touched your eggs benedict and now you want ice cream?"

"I know. I'm sorry." She pulled her hand from his and laced her fingers together in her lap.

"For what? You're not ill, are you?"

"No—no. I'm fine. It's..."

Just say it.

Blurt it out.

Get it over with.

"I fear I've been leading you on."

His forehead creased. "Leading me—"

"Oh, not intentionally. I like you, Daryl—a lot. You've been a great friend."

For a moment, he looked stunned, but seconds later, an inkling of understanding entered his eyes. "Friend, huh?"

"The best." She gave a little, quick nod. "I'd hoped *liking* you would eventually turn into *loving* you, but it hasn't. You're such a good man and deserve someone who truly loves you."

"So...*no* to the rings, then?" His eyes squinted with a twinkle of mischief.

Amanda smiled. "I've always admired how you could extract humor from disappointment."

"Aside from that..." He sheepishly smiled. "I do deserve someone who loves me. I think I've known for quite some time that things were cooling between us. Especially with the return of a—certain person." His genuine smile held a rare sparkle.

She reached across the table and clasped his hand. "And another example of what a fine man you are."

* * *

Ethan and his grandmother sat on the back patio, enjoying their coffee after sharing a late breakfast.

"Poor Amanda," his grandmother said. "To be stranded like that—without even a toothbrush. And she was a trooper the entire time."

"She coped much better than I thought she would."

"And why did you stay the extra two days?" She brought the cup to her lips.

"I needed an extended time in the outdoors. Once you're used to living like that, it becomes part of your DNA." He ran his index finger over the rim of the cup. That excuse was only partly true. His time embedded with the military had taught him the art of revealing only what was necessary for the hearer in the moment.

"So how was it spending two days and two nights all alone with Amanda in an isolated forest?"

"Your effort to throw us together is quite romantic, Grandma." He leaned forward in his chair. "Instead of hints and innuendos, why don't you tell me what you really know about the time I left for college?"

"I've made my feelings on that subject perfectly clear." Her lips pressed together in irritation. "It's not my place to tell you, but Amanda's."

"She did reveal something while we were together."

"And...?"

"Basically, that I didn't come back—said it two or three times, in fact." Ethan sipped his coffee, eyeing her. "She wouldn't tell me much more than that, but she believed I would come back. Not hoped, not wished, but *believed* I would."

"But you did come back. Until you started the internship with *Geographic World*, you came home two or three times that first year or so. After that, you didn't have time to come see us, so we had to travel to you."

"When she says I didn't come back, she means, *for her*."

"I see." His grandmother tapped the rim of her coffee mug. "Then it's time you make her tell you what she's talking about."

"What do you mean *make* her? I've never been able to make Amanda do anything."

"Then you're not the man I thought you were." She shook her head. "You young people today have no imagination."

"What do you propose I do, take her over my knee?"

"Good heavens that archaic practice went out years ago. Your grandfather tried that tactic with me once, and only once." She cradled the mug in her hand. "Trust me, two black eyes later, he never tried that again."

Wow. She must have been a handful. Ethan chuckled and shook his head. He'd never see his sweet grandma the same way again.

"You need to kiss her into submission," she continued. "Your grandfather certainly used that tactic with better success. I have to admit, I rather liked it. At the time, I certainly didn't let *him* know that." She shook a finger. "I didn't cave easily, I can assure you. And then there were the countless times I kissed him into distraction, which ultimately led to *his* submission. Works both ways, you know."

"I didn't know," he said, lifting his brow. "But thank you for enlightening me."

"All that aside, I want you to know, you did nothing wrong establishing your career. It's important for a man to do that when he's young, then he gets married and builds a life with the woman he loves."

"I know."

"Sure, you could have come home, but you were experiencing the opportunity of a lifetime. And you chose career over love. Was that a mistake? I don't think so." She took a quick sip of coffee. "But it doesn't matter what happened in the past. You have *right now*! And if you love Amanda, you'll make something happen soon."

"Easier said than done, Grandma."

"True. You're at another crossroads. It seems to me you have a decision to make. You can choose to either move forward with Amanda or not. Again, it's a question of career, versus love. Choose one or the other, or better yet, find a way to merge them into the life you want."

Ethan retired to his bedroom that evening, sat at his boyhood desk, and opened his laptop. Over the past hour, he'd mulled over his grandmother's advice, but right now, he had work to do. His late-night contact had given him twenty-four hours to write the latest code, then publish it in *Knight Owl*. Ethan's was the last piece needed to plan, set up, and execute the extraction of an Afghan interpreter and his family.

His contact had given him two words, Dahla Dam. He'd already uploaded the other contact's codes and ciphers in the upcoming issue of *Knight Owl* and was now ready to include his contribution, the SMS code. Once he figured out which number on a phone correlated with the letter needed, he typed out the list of numbers to spell Dahla Dam—32445552.326.

The dam was connected to a river in Kandahar. Because of its location, it could be part of the final step in getting this family to safety. Wherever the dam came into their journey, he prayed it would lead to their freedom.

He hit *publish*—his part now done.

Chapter 26

It had been almost a week since Amanda got stranded with Ethan in the State Park. She hadn't seen much of him since and wondered what was happening with the *sale or no sale* of the newspaper. At least, that was the excuse she'd told herself. She'd kept her eye out for him as she went about the week. She shook her head at her adolescent behavior—one day she was doing her best to avoid him, and the next, looking for ways to run into him. She was as bad as a teenage girl with a crush.

She'd spent many hours during the past week, pondering her motivation for kissing him in the tent. She'd been emotionally stirred by his openness about his time embedded with the military. No doubt, that had been part of it, after so many years apart, and then reliving the lake kiss over and over. After sobbing her heart out in his wonderful arms, what choice did she have but to take whatever opportunity arose to kiss him again? From day one, she'd longed to feel his arms around her—to tuck her head against his wonderful broad shoulders—to feel the warmth of his lips on hers.

Truthfully, she'd thought of little else since that night, except for the moment he'd manhandled her. She'd thought plenty about that. Seeing him meet a stranger in the dark of night had conjured up all manner of terrible possibilities. She'd never seen him so angry, and it had frightened her. More than once, she'd found herself reliving her outrage at his roughness when he'd discovered her spying in the forest.

Amanda wore a sleeveless, pink floral cotton dress that hit just above her knees. It was stylish and comfortable and one she felt appropriate for her session with Annie's girls. She had practiced her talk several times for her big Saturday debut. Before the girls arrived, she ran over the bullet points of her talk, *It's Not All About You.*

"Respect—prejudging—own your actions..."

"Relax," Annie said. "You can use your notes, you know."

"I know, but if I'm familiar with the talk, I can give them more eye contact."

"Spoken like a true teacher."

The girl's chatter was infectious as they settled around the table. They all greeted Annie by her first name, but were careful when they approached Amanda, their high school principal. She couldn't help but smile at how formal they'd gotten when they greeted her.

"Relax, girls, you'll get no tests or grades from me, today."

Soft laughter filled the room as Amanda opened the session.

"... After that, Annie is going to take the remainder of the class to introduce you to a new line of makeup specifically designed for teens."

"Now, turn in your notebooks to today's topic, *it's not all about you*. I'm sure someone has said that to you at some point in your life."

The girls all nodded. "Let's talk about what this means

and look at some of the ways we can think differently about others..."

Time flew by, and before Amanda knew it, her part in the morning had ended. While she gathered her notes, Annie closed out the session with a new teen makeup line and tips for applying it.

"You did great, today," Annie said, after the girls had left.

Amanda shrugged with a smile. "Thanks, but I felt it went flat at the beginning. It got better when they started to participate."

"You know teenage girls. They love to talk." Annie grinned. "You're their school principal." Annie placed her hand on Amanda's arm. "We just had to give them time to warm up to you."

"I don't think they were expecting such a serious topic from LNO," Amanda said. "I admit, I'm concerned at how much time the kids spend on their phones and laptops. The tendency to respond to something online without thinking about it first gets them into trouble, or makes them look bad, or causes hurt feelings...oh the list is long, and I'm getting carried away." She cast a sheepish smile.

"It was the best part of today's session, if you ask me." Annie grabbed the extra makeup from the table. "Let's think of some other issues the girls face that we can incorporate into LNO's workshops. Maybe something along the lines of, *the pros and cons of social media*."

Amanda glanced at Annie as they walked out. "This is going to sound way off the wall, but do you know if Levi and Ethan are working together on something?"

"Wow, that is left field. I don't know of anything, but what makes you think there is?"

"Levi picked Ethan and me up from the park on Sunday."

"I know. Levi told me."

"Don't you think that's odd?"

"My husband was elected to protect and serve, remember?"

Amanda shrugged. "I know, but something is going on with Ethan, something undercover or sinister—"

"Sinister?" Annie's eyes widened. "Do you hear yourself?"

Amanda waved a hand in the air. "Forget I said anything."

"Oh, no. You can't shut up now. I'll tell you what. I'm meeting Levi in ten minutes for lunch. Come with me, and you can ask your questions."

* * *

Ethan lowered himself into the seat behind the steering wheel and checked his messages—still no word from his CIA contact. It had been less than a week since he'd posted *Knight Owl* and only three days since the military had put the extraction in motion, but that didn't keep him from worrying.

Six months before, he'd committed to helping the organization. With his latest publication, his verbal contract had ended. The past month, he'd been seriously thinking about extending it, but the weeks spent with Amanda changed all of that. He would leave the group for good, stay in Apalacha Key, and win Amanda back.

His phone buzzed as he adjusted the rearview mirror. The name, John Duncan, came up on the caller ID. "Hey, John, what's up?"

"I know you've decided not to sell, but Bryan Carter with Granger insists on meeting with you about buying *Key News.* Why not meet with him and hear what he has to say, just to get him off my back and yours?"

Ethan inwardly moaned. That was the last thing he needed

right now. "Look, thank him for me, but my answer is the same—not interested."

"Did I mention...he's already on his way?"

"What?"

"Thinks he can convince you if he meets you in person. Seriously, this guy is like a bull in a china shop. I think he just needs to hear it straight from you."

"Where does he think he's meeting me?"

"He'll be staying at the Sea Breeze and said he'll call to set something up after he gets in."

"It would serve him right if I left town." Ethan rubbed his hand around the back of his neck. "Fine, I'll deal with him. Thanks for the heads-up."

Chapter 27

Amanda slid into the booth next to Annie at Pearl's Diner and waited for Levi to join them.

Levi threw Annie a questioning glance upon his arrival. "Amanda, I didn't know you were joining us today."

"I'm not really." She looked at Annie, silently asking for help.

"She's bugged about something, sweetheart," Annie said, "and I told her it was okay to ask you about it."

Amanda glanced between the two and nodded. "That's right, Levi. I just want to ask you a question."

"Sure, go ahead." He slid in the seat opposite.

"Okay... I'll just come right out with it. What's going on between you and Ethan?"

His eyes narrowed, and he glanced between her and Annie. "Uh, nothing."

"Come on, Levi," Amanda said. "I saw that look between you and Ethan when you arrived Sunday morning. I'm not a fool. I know something's going on."

"And that something has nothing to do with me. I'm sorry I can't answer your questions, Amanda. If you want answers, you'll need to ask Ethan."

Annie placed her hand on Amanda's arm and squeezed. "He's right, you know. You and Ethan go way back. He's the one you should talk to."

Amanda left, having gotten nothing from Levi, which didn't surprise her in the least. Levi was an honorable man and would never divulge anything told to him in confidence.

It was a short walk from Pearl's Diner to her house. She let herself in at the side door, kicked off her shoes, and padded into the living room. She tossed the key back in her purse and immediately thought of the day Ethan had teased her for not locking up the house. Since then, she'd made a point to lock not only her house doors but her car as well.

Her phone dinged with a message. It was from Ethan,

I understand you have some questions for me.

"Gee! Thanks, Sheriff." Amanda groaned.

I'll be at your house at three.

* * *

At some point, Ethan planned to answer all of Amanda's questions, but first, his grandmother needed to answer more of his.

He found her sitting in her favorite green-and-yellow striped chair with her knitting needles flying across the yarn. She looked up and smiled when he entered the living room.

"Ethan, what a nice surprise."

He crossed the room and took a seat on the floral sofa across from her. "Let's hope after our discussion, you still feel that way."

"What do that mean?" Her needles paused, then she lowered them to her lap. "Is something wrong?" She went white. "You've settled on a buyer."

"No. As a matter of fact, I've just very recently decided not to sell."

"Oh, Ethan, that's wonderful."

"But only on one condition—that I work things out with Amanda. I refuse to stay in this town and watch her marry Daryl Cleveland."

"All right."

"I'm in the home stretch with Amanda, and I need ammunition."

"You need—"

"I need to know what happened to make Amanda send me away." He edged forward on the seat. "You know something, and however big or small, I demand to know what that something is."

"Okay." His grandmother set the yarn and needles into the basket at her feet. "I'm sure you recall how adamant your dad was about you taking that scholarship."

He nodded.

"Well, it seems his tenacity on the subject didn't stop with you. He also approached Amanda, laid on the guilt and basically blamed her for your refusal to take the scholarship. I don't know how he did it, but he convinced her to persuade you to accept it."

Dumbfounded, he sat back against the cushion. "That's outrageous. And you didn't think to intervene?"

"I found out a year ago when your father told me on his deathbed."

Ethan ran his hands through his hair. "Why didn't you tell me when you found out?"

"I don't know. I thought about it…oh, so many times. If you'd been here, I probably would have."

"I'm surprised at Amanda. How could she go along with him?"

"I'm afraid that's for her to answer."

"Oh, trust me, she will." He stood and turned to leave.

"Don't be so hard on her," his grandmother said. "She was eighteen, and you of all people know how intimidating and manipulative your father could be. There's no telling what he actually said to her."

He knew his father all too well. His grandmother was right. With a hopeful heart, he drove to Amanda's bungalow with ammunition. He hoped it would be enough.

CHAPTER 28

Ethan stood at Amanda's front door and knocked. He waited, then knocked again. Her car was in the drive, so he assumed she was at home. He walked to the side kitchen door and knocked a third time. She didn't answer, so he tried the handle. The door opened.

He poked his head through the opening. "Amanda, you in there?" he called out as he stepped inside.

"Just a minute—just a minute."

When he finally saw her, he could tell she'd been asleep—hair tousled, barefoot, and slightly annoyed. She was beautiful.

"How did—"

"Your door was unlocked," he said. "I thought I warned you about that. I could have been anybody."

"I'm not in the mood for a lecture." She started walking back into the living room. "What do you want?"

"I understand you have questions?"

She stopped and turned back to him. I lovely pink flush covered her cheeks. At least she had the grace to blush.

She folded her arms. "Not any you're likely to answer."

"So, you asked the sheriff instead?"

"I did." She ran a pink-polished toe across the pine flooring. "Unfortunately, he wasn't forthcoming, either."

"It so happens I have questions, too. For instance, why were you so insistent that I take that scholarship?"

"I thought we already settled this."

"Not to my satisfaction," he said. "There's something else you're not telling me." *Just tell me what he said to you.* "We've settled everything except for, *why*."

Amanda cocked her head to the side. "I told you, that's a question for your grandmother."

"And she tells me to ask you—and round and round it goes."

He stepped toward her, and she stepped back. "Running away?" He glanced around the room. "Trust me, you won't get far, at least not until I get some answers. My grandmother told me I should *make you* tell me what's been going on in that mind of yours. Not bad advice, now that I think of it."

"Huh." She lifted her chin. "I'd like to see you try."

"Is that an invitation?" he moved closer.

"Stay away from me, Ethan."

"Maybe I should take you back out in the forest again, put you inside a six-by-five tent, and continue this discussion. At least there I had your undivided attention."

She dropped her gaze and ran her hands down the sides of her dress. Good, he had her right where he wanted her. He pulled her unresistingly into his arms and planted a quick, forceful kiss on her lips.

He lifted his head and held her slightly away from him. At the sudden, sweet longing in her eyes, he groaned and kissed her again, deeply, slowly, and with purpose. She wound her arms around his neck as he moved from her mouth to her soft cheek, brushing his lips along her jaw. She tilted her head, and he continued his attention down, gently caressing her neck.

His phone buzzed from inside his back pocket, jarring him back to reality.

Blast it.

He lifted his head. "Sorry, darling, I'm expecting a call."

Amanda clung to him, all dreamy-eyed and happy. "It's okay."

A quick glance at his phone revealed a text from Bryan Carter, listing the time and place for their meeting. He should leave the man hanging, but he wanted the decision to be over with. He was keeping the paper. The sooner he met with and sent Bryan Carter away, the sooner he could prove to Amanda he was home for good. All he wanted was to start their new life together.

He shoved his phone into his pocket, pulled her back into his arms, and lowered his mouth to hers. Seconds later, he lifted his head and placed his fingers on her mouth. "Hold my place until I get back."

She clasped her lower lip between her teeth and nodded. The golden smile she gave him squeezed his heart.

He cupped her face in his hands. "I'll be back as soon as I can. We still have a lot to talk about." He released her, tapped her nose, and made his way for the door.

"Where are you going?"

"I have to deal with a bull in a china shop."

* * *

Since it sounded like Ethan could be a while, Amanda decided for a quick stroll along the boulevard. The short walk from her bungalow to the gulf took only a few minutes. The sun danced across the emerald water in the distance and seemed to reflect her soaring happiness.

Feeling like a breathless girl of eighteen, she placed her fingers to her mouth and smiled. Could this really be happening? He had a lot to tell her, he'd said. That breathtaking kiss could only mean one thing—Ethan was not selling the paper and was staying there. A warm glow flowed through her, making her blissfully happy.

She got to the crosswalk at 30A and spotted a short, stocky man dressed in a tan linen jacket and white pants.

"Hello, you seem lost." She smiled, assuming he was a tourist.

He turned toward her. "Not so much lost as mesmerized by that gorgeous blue-green water."

"Our beaches are some of the most beautiful in the world. And if you have time and like seafood, I can recommend Cole's Oyster Bar on Market Street."

"Thank you. I'm here on business and only for one night, but I appreciate the recommendation."

"Anything else I can help you with?"

"I have a meeting in a few minutes at the Sea Breeze Hotel, but I was hoping Third Avenue was nearby."

"It is." Amanda lifted her arm and pointed ahead. "Stay on this road, and when you get to the next stop sign, go left. That's Third."

"Wonderful. I'm anxious to see *Key Newspaper*. I understand the building it's in is quite historic."

"It is," she said. "Are you an architect?"

"No, I'm here to finalize a deal with the owner."

Her world suddenly spun. That made no sense. Had Ethan changed his mind about not selling...again?

"Oh... Well... I must get going," she said.

"Of course. Sorry to have kept you."

All she could do was nod. Her mind reeled with confusion —her sudden misery was like a steel weight. She blinked away tears as anger and disappointment rushed to the forefront of her mind. She would not cry. Fifteen minutes earlier, she'd basked in Ethan's arms. Had she misunderstood those sweet moments of affection?

She'd felt certain he was going to stay and make a go of it. *And ten years ago, you felt certain he'd come back for you, too.* She covered her face with her hands.

The pleasure of the afternoon evaporated. The last thing Amanda wanted now was a nice walk along the beach. A knot of bitter disappointment formed in her chest. Frowning, she watched the man stride away. If she'd known who he was and why he was in town, she may not have been quite so helpful.

She crossed 30A and headed for her little bungalow by the sea. She pulled a key from her purse and unlocked the side door. She slumped across the room and threw herself onto the sofa. Sighing, she picked up the pink throw pillow and hugged it to her chest. Hot tears slipped down her cheeks, and she gulped hard. She pressed her face to the pillow and yielded to the compulsive sobs that shook her.

Still clutching the pillow, she lifted her head and angrily swiped away her tears. She glanced around her neatly organized living room, tidy as always with everything in its place.

Was that it? Was she now back to her boring predictable life? Was she now doomed for spinsterhood? Her only companions—a house filled with cats? Was she to live out her life as a high school principal, receive a gold watch for her years of effort, only to retire on a teacher's pension?

Admit it, Ethan Knight brought life and love back into your safely, ordered world.

Love, real *lasting* love, was what she'd been missing all of the years since he'd gone away. His return had awakened her from a methodical existence. And now, it looked like he was leaving again. She'd been a fool to believe this time would be any different. She'd waited for him once before but wouldn't make that mistake a second time.

She was no longer a young, foolish, bright-eyed teenager. She was a high school principal, a schoolmarm, and a schoolmarm she'd always be. She marched to her bedroom, stood in front of her mirror, and twisted her hair into a tight knot.

She'd go to him and make it clear he was free to leave and live his own life. And this time, she'd *mean* it.

* * *

Ethan strode into the hotel's bar and spotted Bryan Carter at the counter.

"Just the man I want to see," Bryan said. "Bartender, pour this man a drink."

"No thank you." Ethan lifted a hand to the waiter. "Bryan, both Duncan and I have made it perfectly clear I'm not selling, and there's nothing you can do or say, and no amount of money to make me change my mind." Ethan's quick-and-to-the-point statement left no room for further discussion.

Bryan sat at the bar looking dumbfounded—clearly unused to hearing the word *no*, and in such an unforeseen manner. Ethan stuck out his hand, and the man slowly took it.

"Wouldn't you at least like to hear my presentation?" Bryan asked.

"That would only waste both of our time. Our business here is over. Before you leave, may I suggest a stroll on our beautiful beach, followed by the hotel restaurant's famous seafood platter. Now. I hate to be abrupt, but I have another pressing appointment."

With that, Ethan walked out of the restaurant and never looked back.

Ethan climbed into his BMW and turned the ignition. He put the car in reverse, backed out of his spot, then headed toward the exit. He stopped at the cross-street and checked his phone. He noticed a text from his CIA contact. His heart thumped and he held his breath as he opened the message—the words were simple and to the point.

Package delivered safe and sound.

Ethan let out his tightly held breath and leaned back against the seat headrest. The family was finally safe—free, and he'd played an important part in their rescue.

Enormous relief spread through his veins, and for the first time in days, he could relax. More than that, he was now finished with his commitment to the military and free to share everything with Amanda. It was time to clear the air with her in every respect.

CHAPTER 29

Ethan tapped on Amanda's side door, turned the handle, and entered.

Amanda swung around. "So, what? We don't wait to be invited in now?"

"Sorry, I—" He stopped in the middle of the kitchen and stared. "Have you been crying? And what's up with your hair?"

"How I wear my hair is none of your concern."

He lifted a brow. "And the crying?"

"Also none of your concern."

"I see." He stuffed his hands into his pockets and studied her. He'd been gone for less than an hour, but something had obviously gone wrong while he'd been away.

Her mouth spread into a thin-lipped smile. "I understand congratulations are in order."

He narrowed his eyes. "What for?"

"I met your buyer today. He was quite eager to finalize the details of the sale with you. He seems like the nicest man and will probably be a great addition to the town." She spun away and sat down in one of the kitchen chairs.

"Are you serious?" Ethan gaped at her. "Is that what has you so riled up?"

She smiled brightly and flitted her right hand through the air. "On the contrary. I mean, if it's what *you* want, and if it's good for the paper, why not?"

Ethan slid out one of the chairs and straddled it. He rested his arms along the back and regarded her with steely amusement and a slight smile. "You know what this reminds me of?"

"What?"

"The day you assured me that Syracuse University was too good of an opportunity to turn down."

Her smile faded. She swallowed and licked her lips.

"I seem to recall you insisting how good it would be for my career. So now what? Is this your standard, go-to method to get rid of me? Because I have to tell you, that won't wash a second time."

She lifted her chin and gave him her no-nonsense, principal stare. "It's only my way of saying I want the best for you as I've always wanted." Her patronizing tone was not lost on him. "Ten years ago, Syracuse University *was* the best for you. And today, if selling the paper and moving on with your life is the best for you, then that's what I want, too."

He slowly shook his head. "Such a martyr."

"Excuse me?"

"You heard me. What makes you think I'm selling the paper? Some aggressive buyer shows up and you believe him instead of me? I thought I made it perfectly clear that I wasn't selling."

She folded her arms and lifted a brow.

"Okay, fine. I hadn't completely made the decision when we last talked, but that's because I've been forever trying to read you. Can't you tell what I've been trying to say to you?"

"Oh, so now I'm supposed to be clairvoyant, is that it?"

"A little bit of women's intuition is all I'm hoping for here."

She made a move to get up. He grabbed her arm. "Sit. Down. We'll either deal with this now or back in that little pup tent. Your choice."

She pinned him with something close to belligerence and plopped back in her chair.

He dropped his hand from her arm. "Something keeps bothering me about our conversation in the forest. I feel like we're forever going in circles as if you're still avoiding telling me something."

She gave him a blank stare. Her way of saying, he'd get nothing from her.

"You parroted my father's very own words."

"Are you accusing me of something?" She fisted a wad of her dress.

"If the shoe fits," he replied.

"Why are we still talking about this?" Frustration sparkled in her tawny eyes. "That was years ago."

"And it's still between us today. It's in everything you *don't* say—it's what you leave out that I'd like to hear. I think it's time you tell me what happened."

She sat back straight, perfectly rigid.

"If it helps any, my grandmother told me of my father's involvement."

"She...she told you?" Amanda's shoulders slumped, and she physically sagged.

Ethan quickly placed both hands on her arms. "My father never punched a soul in his life, but he hit plenty with his words."

"That, I can personally attest to," she said in a weary voice.

"What did he say to you?"

She eyed him with a miserable gaze. "You're not going to like it."

"I already don't like it." He ran his hands up her arms to rest on her shoulders while keeping his gaze on her face. "It's important I know why you went along with him."

Tears glistened in her eyes. "Do you remember the day on the beach when we mapped out our future together?"

"I do." He lowered his hands, fisting them in his lap.

"We were so much in love. You—our plans to go to college together, to marry, meant the whole world to me."

"Me, too." He nodded.

"All the dreams of teenagers in love, right?"

"But—"

"That night, your father came to see me. I thought it was you and flung open the door, only to see him standing there.

"The first words out of his mouth were, *what do you think you're doing girl, keeping my son from his future—his success—his dreams, all the things he's longed for and worked for since he was a boy?*" She pressed her fingers to her forehead. "He continued to expound, piling on more reasons that aren't all that important now."

Ethan knew how manipulative his dad could be, but what he'd done to Amanda went beyond the pale.

"Back then," she continued, "I was easily intimidated, but I flat told him, no—told him he needed to tell *you* those things. He said he had been telling you and that you wouldn't listen." She threw up her arms. "He told me you'd been overly influenced by me. That you were throwing your future away for a short-sighted, high school romance.

"To be fair, he assured me that if ours was the real thing, you'd come back to me. And we've already established how well that worked out. Anyway, that's what he said on his *first* visit. After the third time, I...I agreed to do it."

"Why?" Ethan lifted his hands to cup her face. "Why didn't you just come to me?"

She burst into tears, and he dropped his hands from her face. "Because I believed you wouldn't listen to me, either. That you would tell me no, just like you'd been telling him. Then I saw your face, the crushing blow my words had done to you. I realized in that moment you didn't think I loved you."

She pulled a tissue from the box on the table and blew her nose. "And then I thought, if he doesn't think I love him, he'll go." Amanda lifted a sorrowful gaze, her lashes wet with tears. "I mean, how could a girl who loved you, planned a future with you, send you away—with a smile no less?" She wrung her hands. "I just stood there and let you believe it."

Tears slipped down her cheeks, and she brushed them away. "To justify my own behavior, I began to wonder if he could be right. Oh, not in his method, but scholarships like that didn't come around very often. When you got that summer internship with *Geographic World*, I knew your dad had been right."

Ethan shot to his feet. "I should've known—should've known it was all him." He began to pace. "I suspected as much when you let slip that *we* wanted the best—" He abruptly stopped, sat back down, and took both her hands in his. "I am so, so sorry." He lifted one hand, cupped the side of her face, and brushed an errant tear away with his thumb. "Are you all right?"

She pulled her hands free, grabbed another tissue, and blew her nose. "I guess it was time I finally dealt with all that teenage drama." She sniffed and lifted a watery smile to his face. "It's funny how things just build up over time."

"We were teenagers."

"That seems to be the answer for all of our woes."

"And the answer as to why you've been angry with me." He tipped up her chin with his finger.

"What?"

"You know, for not coming back for you."

"I'm not angry over that. I've never been angry over that—hurt yes, but not angry."

"Then what—?" Light suddenly dawned—*of course*. It was all starting to make sense.

"That meeting in your office when you alluded to giving up something," he said. "That's why you were angry. It was about what you gave up."

Her expression darkened. He could see she wasn't happy about where their conversation was going. Her tawny eyes flashed with determination, reminding him of the day she'd let it all fly at the school parking lot. She jumped to her feet and scowled at him.

"Yes... I gave something up. *You*." She jabbed her finger into his chest. "So your photojournalism dreams could come true, *not* for some meaningless, online dribble."

Of course, she'd been proud of him and had painstakingly followed his award-winning journalism, only to see it disappear when he'd created *Knight Owl*. He recalled the day at the Green Parrot when he'd told her she'd always put others' needs before her own. In sending him away, she'd done just that. It had been okay to give up her one true love for his success but not for that *tabloid rag*.

"I kept thinking...what's the point?" She threw up her hands. "If your talent was to go to the lowest denominator, then at least we could've had a life together, instead of ten *long* years apart. Once, I even tried to work one of those insane puzzles of yours—Impossible!"

Spellbound, he watched her rant and listened as she finally said what she'd been holding back—and it was fantastic. "You actually tried to figure one out?" He regarded her with amused wonder.

"Yes!"

Even then, she'd tried to make sense of his work—of what he'd done. If her actions weren't a sign of love, then he didn't know what was.

"I admit, most of it is a tabloid, a rag, and meaningless dribble," he teased with a soft grin, "but with one *really* big difference."

With a slight shake of her head, she eyed him with a combination of confusion and curiosity.

"I love how you still fight for what you think is best for me." Ethan adored Amanda more in that moment than ever before. She'd championed him like the day she'd fought for Annie and Levi in the parking lot. "Please sit back down, Mandy. I promise I'm almost through."

She slowly sat with a movement of resignation.

"Remember when I told you about the stress of being embedded with the military and how I decided to leave?"

She nodded.

"About seven months ago, the CIA approached me to write code, within a story, that would be used to communicate information like simple directions, pickup times, and places. The info would be used to extract our people who'd been left behind in war-torn parts of the world.

"It was supposed to be a one-time thing, but I was really good at it. The government approached me again, asking if I would commit to do more.

"I realized, here was a way I could still help—a way I could be part of the action without having to risk my life or my sanity to do it. For six months, I had experienced the devastation of war and had written about it. Now, I had the opportunity to use my gift to save lives. That's when I came up with the idea for *Knight Owl*, a simple online paper filled with lifesaving information. Who would ever suspect that?"

A soft gasp escaped her. "So, you stayed involved, but from a safe distance."

"Exactly. Everything we did was top-secret. That's why I couldn't share any of it with you."

A glint of wonder filled her eyes. "Why now?"

"Because I just finished my last job with them. I'm no longer a part of *Knight Owl*."

"I don't understand. You created it."

"Yes, I did. At first it was totally my baby. The military contractors explained what they needed, then gave me the information pertinent for each mission. I put that information in the form of a code for the parties involved. I created everything from a story, a fake ad, a poem, or a game. It was never the same from one publication to the next, and the code was always different, depending on what was printed.

"In a matter of months, the publication became way too much for one person. So, we created a small network intended for long-term use without being dependent on any one individual. That way the work of *Knight Owl* would continue as long as it was needed."

"Who was the man in the forest?" She lightly fingered a loose tendril of hair on her cheek.

"My CIA contact. These people are extremely secretive, and this particular person is known for his explosive personality. If he'd known of your presence, we may have had to change the entire plan to rescue this Afghan family."

"Why meet in the woods?' She clasped her hands together. "Why not use the Internet to communicate?"

"We do use the Internet—encoded messages—the works, but two weeks ago, I received an encrypted message that the system had been compromised. We couldn't take the chance to send the information as usual. So, we decided to meet here in Apalacha Key."

"That's incredible."

"Since I was going to be with the kids in the State Park, I thought that would be the perfect place to meet my contact." He ran his finger down the bridge of her nose. "I just didn't know I was going to have extra baggage along the way."

She flushed an adorable pink. "And the sheriff?"

Ethan cupped her face with his hands and gave her a quick kiss. "He was in the loop from the very beginning. I brought this to his town, and I wanted backup in case something went wrong."

"I can hardly imagine what that's like," she said, breathlessly. "To rescue someone is extraordinary."

"The rush is amazing—every time. The first extraction was similar to this one. We not only saved one man's life, but also that of his entire family. After months of death and carnage, this was light instead of darkness for me. And if I were to stay involved, this was how I had to do it—the only way I *could* do it."

"Wow." The word tumbled from her lips like a sigh and made him smile.

Ethan stood. "Enough talking. Can we go someplace a little more comfortable?"

* * *

Amanda's heart soared with eager warmth. Ethan took her hand and led her out of the kitchen, through the living room, to the backyard deck. The sun had just set casting a golden glow over the early evening sky. He sat on the plush outdoor sofa, pulled her down beside him, and hitched her close to his side.

"That's more like it," he whispered against her ear. With his left hand, he unclipped the topknot from her head, and her hair tumbled to her shoulders. "Please don't ever put your gorgeous hair up in that unsightly bun."

A soft laugh escaped her. "I knew it would annoy you." She pecked little kisses along his jaw.

Hoot-hoot.

Amanda tilted her head and sucked in a breath. "Listen... an owl."

Hoot-hoot.

"Haunting, yet beautiful," she whispered.

"Silent and watchful," he added.

She gazed up at him. "Why did you choose the name *owl*, for your online magazine."

"Oh, so it's a magazine now?" He grinned.

She gave him an impish smile. "I feel like I've disparaged it enough. If you only knew half of what I really thought about it over the past six months, it would make even *you* blush."

Eyes glistening with humor, he lowered his head and gave her a generous peck on the lips.

"To answer your question, the owl symbolizes different things depending on the culture. But for me, the symbols—wisdom, mystery, intelligence and protection—made the owl the perfect mascot for what our band of mighty rescuers do."

"I can see that." She nodded. "What else?"

"They're masters of camouflage and their feathers are

unique, enabling them to fly almost silently. They're highly adaptable, specialized predators, with extraordinary night vision and hearing, all of which make up their intelligent and strategic approach to hunting."

Hoot-hoot-hoooooot.

"I think he's agreeing with you," she chuckled.

"I think so, too," Ethan laughed.

"I had no idea owls were such remarkable birds," she said. "Their uniqueness embodies all the attributes needed to plan and execute your rescue missions."

"Exactly." His beautiful eyes scanned her face as he ran his finger along the left side of her cheek. "Is that all you wish to know?"

"For the time being."

He shifted her slightly so that they faced each other. The warmth of his arms—his nearness made her senses spin. "Ethan?"

"Mmm?"

"Now that you've finished with the *Owl*, what are you planning to do?"

"You know..." He feathered kisses along her shoulder. "I was just about to get to that."

He lifted his head. "The publisher at *Geographic World* has been after me to come back for some time now. In the beginning, I'd only planned to take a short sabbatical from them."

"That's wonderful news."

"Yep, they offered me another contract, but I turned it down."

"Why?" Her voice rang with the dismay she felt.

Ethan's firm lips slowly lifted into a half smile as if he alone held a secret he would soon reveal. "I told them I could only work freelance as I was planning to get married and wanted my wife to be able to travel with me."

"Really?" Amanda sighed, and practically swooned over the idea. She wound her arms around his neck. "Who's the lucky girl?"

"A completely maddening woman—exasperating to the core, but the most adorable creature on every other level." He pinned her with an amused stare and shook his head.

"Ooooh, I like her already. She sounds *perfect* for you."

He chuckled and gave her a big squeeze. "What would you say to a little world-traveling in the summers? I figured since your schedule is so *predictable* you might be able to work that out."

"I think that could be arranged." She rested her cheek against his shoulder and gazed up at him.

Ethan brushed a lock of hair off her forehead. "Happy?"

"You know I am."

His mouth captured hers, and she drank in the sweetness of his kiss.

A moment later, she shifted slightly and encircled her arms around his waist. She snuggled into him, pressing her head against his chest. "What made you change your mind about selling the paper?" she asked.

"It was a combination of things." He gently rubbed his hand up and down her back. "My grandmother's disappointment, my growing concern for our staff, and information I gleaned over the past many weeks. I finally had to ask myself if I was willing to walk away from four generations of Knight-family newsmen and everything my ancestors had created. And the answer was no."

She rose up and lightly pecked his cheek. "I never stopped loving you. That day in the parking lot...I knew it, even then."

"Ahh, the infamous school-parking-lot scene." His eyes held a teasing light.

"What about you?" She trailed her finger along his jaw. The humor in his gaze, clear evidence he knew exactly what she was asking.

"That event was actually a turning point for me as well." He planted a swift kiss on her mouth. "Everything you meant to me came back that day—my beautiful, avenging angel protecting Anna Delany and her sheriff. And yes... I knew in that moment that I still loved you."

"I knew it." She grinned.

"And I decided then and there, to do everything I could to win you back." His compelling blue eyes crinkled at the corners as he smiled down at her, evidence of every ounce of his love and affection.

"My dearest, darling, Ethan. I love you so much." With her arms still wrapped snuggly around his waist, she gave him a fierce hug.

"I've waited so long to hear you say those words again, but I just have one more question."

Amanda released his waist with an exaggerated groan. "You and your questions. What could you possibly want to know now?"

"What are you planning to do about *Mr.* Vanilla?"

"Poor Daryl." In a state bordering pure happiness, she wound her arms around his neck. "He never had a chance after you came back. How could I settle for vanilla when I can have cherry cream cheese?"

If you'd like to read the first two books in my *Like No Other* series, just click on the links below.

Hawke's Nest - Like No Other, Book 1
https://amzn.to/3UieG0r

Hawke's Nest, follows supermodel Annie Dell in the aftermath of a misinformed and false scandal, she is forced to seek refuge from paparazzi filled New York City, to a small beach town in Florida for her best friend's wedding, where she get's herself off on the wrong side of the county Sheriff, the handsome Levi Hawke. Will everything just blow over? Or will a hurricane quite literally blow her away?

Eagle Eye - Like No Other, Book 2
https://amzn.to/3tWlKF1

Eagle Eye, follows up-and-coming teen fashion designer Jill Jeffrey, when a case of mistaken identity and misinterpreted motives leads to a career-ending article by the notoriously honest Eagle Eye. Jill finds herself in hot water, but can her new journalist friend, Cameron Phillips help her clear her name? Or was he the one who drug it through the mud in the first place?

Thank you for reading!

Dear Reader,

I hope you enjoyed ***Knight Owl, Like No Other- Book 3***. I had so much fun writing Amanda and Ethan's story!

I need to ask a favor. As you probably know, reviews can be hard to come by. And as a reader your feedback is so important. If you're so inclined, I'd love an honest review of *Knight Owl.* It doesn't have to be long or fancy. :) One or two sentences is fine.

If you have time, here's a link to my author page on Amazon. You can check out all my books here:

http://www.amazon.com/-/e/B0077AG3ZM

You can find out more about ***Like No Other*** and how it began in *Hawke's Nest* and *Eagle Eye*, the first two books in the series.

In gratitude,
Darcy Flynn

www.ingramcontent.com/pod-product-compliance
Lightning Source LLC
Chambersburg PA
CBHW061530250926
52052CB00010B/2874
9781941925270